# Devil's Harvest

Frank G. Slaughter

PUBLISHED BY POCKET BOOKS NEW YORK

## DEVIL'S HARVEST

Doubleday edition published March, 1963

POCKET BOOK edition published April, 1964

4th printing........................April, 1976

**This POCKET BOOK edition includes every word contained in
the original, higher-priced edition. It is printed from brand-
new plates made from completely reset, clear, easy-to-read type.
POCKET BOOK editions are published by
POCKET BOOKS,
a division of Simon & Schuster, Inc.,
A GULF+WESTERN COMPANY
630 Fifth Avenue,
New York, N.Y. 10020.
Trademarks registered in the United States
and other countries.**

# 1.

THE scene beneath the wing-tips had taken on added meaning for John Merchant with each turn of the propellers. Now, while the plane continued to fly almost due north, the turgid greens of the rain forests had yielded to stands of teak and pine, to the gleam of waterfalls, to peaks lifted boldly above high meadows. Dead ahead, John could see the first real mountains—and the saw-toothed *séracs* that marked the homestretch of this two-hour flight. Already he could pick out landmarks from a day when these same mountains had been the boundaries of his world.

The Dakota banked to escape an air pocket, and he glanced again at the girl in the denim coveralls who sat at the controls. His pilot, he gathered, was still in no mood to consider direct questions, much less to answer them.

When they had met on the airstrip at Chiang Mai, he had been startled that Indra Lal, and not Chan Thornton, had met him—and more than a little gratified. His pleasure had soon been dashed in her total lack of warmth—but he could understand, all too well, the restraints a five-year absence had imposed on them both. It was Indra's right to forget they had once been something more than friends. Purists might insist it was her duty.

"Does this seem like a homecoming, Doctor?"

"Not so far." He spoke the falsehood boldly, determined to break the barrier by frontal assault. "It won't, until you remember my first name."

"I'm sorry, John. Will it help if you call me Indra?"

The concession, he saw, was deliberate. It was small comfort to know her cool poise was defensive.

"First names were easier in those days—when we were still young."

"I was old enough to teach in the nursing school."

1

"You were always a special protégée at the hospital. Now, it seems, you've turned aviator as well."

"Chan taught me to fly years ago," said Indra Lal. "We share our skills at Muong Toa."

*Share your skills, and learn others.* That, Dr. John Merchant reflected, has always been Oscar Thornton's way. About to put the memory into words, he curbed the impulse. Papa Oscar was still alive: he had not intended to think of him in the past tense. Glancing again at the girl, he was glad he had held his tongue. After two hours in the narrow cockpit, he was still unnerved by the rediscovery of her beauty—a deep charm not even the shapeless flying suit could disguise.

"It was good of you to come at once," said Indra.

"You aren't the only one who owes everything to Papa Oscar."

Again, the girl seemed to ignore an effort at camaraderie deliberately. "You'll see the hospital when we break through the cloud cover. I'm circling the field for a while. We can't risk a landing until the wind dies." Her voice had softened a trifle, as she continued to study the fleecy mass of vapor below. "Does it seem real *now?*"

"So far, I'm floating between two worlds, with a foot in neither."

"Can't you believe you were in San Francisco two days ago?"

"Without too much effort, Indra: thanks to my job, I'm hardly a stranger to the jet age. It's much harder to realize the Enchanted Valley's below us."

"I hope this visit won't mean a setback in your work."

"My experiments are in good hands. In any case, they can wait. It's Papa Oscar I'm thinking of at this moment."

"Look down, John. You'll find things much as you remember them."

He saw that they had penetrated the cloud cover. The valley where Dr. Oscar Thornton's word had been law for a generation revealed itself gradually, with all its well-loved contours intact. His eye darted to the white-roofed hospital buildings, to the workshops and the model farm. There, just inside the kampong gate, were the guesthouse and the direc-

2

tor's residence, each in its nest of bamboo and flame-trees. . . . The low-eaved building near the clinic, John thought, must be Chan Thornton's new laboratory.

The airstrip (it seemed larger than he recalled) lay to the south of the gate, and the native village that clustered there. To the east were the terraced rice paddies with their irrigation dam: the low hills beyond were dotted with the high-stilted huts of Meo herders. John could just discern far up the valley, half-lost in shadowy mountain masses, the tan-colored walls of the Buddhist monastery. Farther still, a few miles short of China's Yunnan Province, were the two escarpments called the Gates of Hell: in the late afternoon light, they were only an inky silhouette.

"I'm glad your world has changed so little, Indra." His voice, John knew, was a trifle husky: that scene below their wings was a memory come true, a page from a book of bright yesterdays. Even those two shadowed *massifs* in the distance could not distort its air of peace. Accepting remoteness as their due, the people of Muong Toa had always considered their valley as enchanted as its name. While Oscar Thornton ruled, it had been easy to close one's mind to what lay beyond the border.

"We'll stay airborne a bit longer," said Indra Lal. "The wind dies down with evening—as you no doubt remember."

She banked sharply with the decision. In a space of seconds, the plane had broken its tentative contact with the land. Oscar Thornton's domain had assumed toy-town dimensions again, before it merged with the misty greens of his valley.

Muong Toa, John told himself, was real enough. He could accept the fact that Papa Oscar was facing a terminal illness there: the brief description Indra had given him of the old doctor's plight suggested that his long journey of mercy was futile. Yet he had not even paused for thought when he answered Chan Thornton's summons. Despite the uncertain future that shadowed it, the Enchanted Valley remained his lodestar, the only real home he had ever known.

From a rear seat of the plane, the chatter of an Olivetti portable resumed its brisk tempo. John noticed the sound resentfully. Intent on this first, disturbing contact with the past, he had forgotten their passenger, half-hidden by a stack of airfreight.

Mirrors above the instrument panel gave a perfect view of the cabin behind the pilots' seats. Alexander Wilde, John saw, was deep in his work. The wrinkled, too-tight seersucker coat he wore accented an almost porcine bulk. The moon-face behind prodigious horn-rims, the smiling, loose-lipped mouth and the air of massive ease recalled a sheep dog, adept at herding flocks to the corral of his choosing. Lex Wilde, as he was known to millions of newspaper readers, had perfected his surface manner long ago. John knew it concealed an uncanny flair for headlines in the making, a tireless ability to manipulate facts to fit a thesis.

Only yesterday, Wilde had picked up his trail in Bangkok, after a nimble chase that had brought him, quite literally, across half the world. Front pages in America had already announced that Oscar Thornton was dying in his remote Asian valley. American editors knew that Dr. John Merchant was en route to attend this almost mythical figure, whose work among primitive peoples ranked with that of Schweitzer. . . . Lex Wilde was not the only international journalist who had pounced on John while he awaited clearance in Bangkok—but none of the others had boasted credentials from a London news agency, entitling him to fly over territory occupied by the Pathet Lao.

When John had boarded his jet at Bangkok, Alexander Wilde had occupied the seat beside him. At the north Thailand center of Chiang Mai, Lex had eased his heavy frame into the Dakota, as calmly as though the plane were his personal transport. Now, almost as though he felt the probe of John's eyes in the mirror, Wilde spoke through a crescendo of typing:

"I hate to bear down when you're busy, Miss Lal. You're *sure* there's no chance for an interview with Oscar Thornton?"

John cut in before Indra could answer: the taut line of her lips was warning enough:

"You must know that answer by now, Lex."

4

"Dr. Thornton made magnificent news in his heyday," said the journalist. "He's still news, now he's dying."

"He was still alive, when we asked in Chiang Mai."

"Even if he recovers, a summing-up would be invaluable."

"Sure you aren't composing that now?" John asked.

"I'd resent that remark, if I didn't know you." Lex ripped a page from the machine and moved forward. "Thanks to a hungry press in the States, I *am* writing my next column. It's partly about you. Want to try it for size?"

"Are you sure I should?"

"If the shortwave transmitter is operating in Muong Toa," said Wilde, "this will appear in two hundred American papers tomorrow—to say nothing of Honolulu and Hong Kong. I think you should glance through it, if only for your peace of mind."

Skimming Lex's hand-tailored substitute for news, John felt his hackles rise at the first words. It was a dateline only Wilde would have used to head a story:

April 24, 1962
Airborne, north of Bangkok.

Today's column takes off from the lounge of the Hotel des Deux Mondes, in a city Conrad tells us has always held the true colors of the East. It was in Bangkok that my trail crossed with Dr. John Merchant's, the microbiologist whose research in leukemia and algal culture has made his name famous among scientists on three continents.

Lex, absorbed in notes, gave no sign that his prose was under appraisal. Tomorrow's column, John perceived, was a good example of Wilde's flair for making the exotic seem familiar as a supermarket, and almost as nourishing. Fixing the pages to a clipboard on the instrument panel (so that Indra could scan them if she chose) he read on:

Dr. Merchant's reason for leaving his San Francisco laboratory is a tragic one. When I joined him, on this final stage of a long journey, he admitted his chance to

5

save the life of Dr. Oscar Thornton, known as Papa Oscar to a generation of grateful Lao and Burmese, seemed remote indeed.

"So long as a shred of hope remains," he told me, "I must do what I can."

Last week, when the world learned that Oscar Thornton was critically ill, readers with long memories found themselves turning back for a reappraisal, your correspondent among them. Even before the start of World War II, the now-venerable doctor had won universal fame for the self-sustaining Utopia he had created in his mountain defile—near the point where the borders of Laos, Burma and China meet.

Dr. Thornton's success in the field of cultural anthropology, an interest that first drew him to this region, needs no repeating here—but it is the creation of this primitive Eden that made headlines in the past, when it was named, for good reason, the Enchanted Valley. Today, we are told, his Eden still flourishes in Communism's shadow. The fact has been explained, by Dr. Thornton himself, as a freak of geography. Outsiders could not help wondering how much he had surrendered to the enemy, to preserve his freedom.

When asked his views on the Valley's apparent autonomy, Dr. Merchant spoke in ringing affirmatives.

"Dr. Thornton is an old friend," he said. "So is his son Chan. Their hospital and farm-projects at Muong Toa are their lifework—and a monument to their dedication. You can be sure they will go on as before."

John turned to Indra—but she did not meet his glance, though he knew she had read every word of Wilde's preheated prose, as carefully and as resentfully as he. Resisting a desire to rip the pages to bits, he passed them to the journalist without comment.

"Edit what you like," said Wilde. "I'm used to blue pencils."

"It's your column, Lex, not mine."

"All I've said is fair comment." Wilde leaned forward to address Indra. "Do *you* think I'm unfair?"

"How can you form these opinions, sight unseen?"

"Opinions are part of my job, Miss Lal. After all, you *have* existed a long time on an enemy border."

"You'll soon see how well we've fared," said Indra crisply. "If you're open-minded, you'll admit we've kept our independence. Fasten your seat belts, both of you. We're going in."

The rebuke, for all its restrained phrasing, had been absolute. Silence fell in the cockpit. It was broken abruptly by the hurricane of the motor, gunned to combat the upward thrust of the wind. Already the Asian earth was rushing to meet them at a dizzy speed.

"That's an odd geological formation to the north," Wilde said. "I mean the two rock pinnacles. Is there really a space between them, or do my eyes deceive me?"

"There's a space, Lex. A hundred yards wide, at most."

"It must lead into China."

"Your geography's as good as your eyesight," John said. "It's the only pass in that mountain wall this side of Burma."

"Anything so strategic should have a name."

"It does—the Gates of Hell. The natives have called it that since the days of Genghis Khan."

"The Gates of Hell, guarding an Enchanted Valley." The journalist whistled softly. "I must do a piece on that: the symbolism's perfect."

"You aren't the first poet to note the narrow boundary that separates hell from heaven," John said dryly.

There was no time for more. The plane, jolting into a fair three-point landing, had made contact with the airstrip.

Anxious to determine his patient's exact condition, John had gone straight to the hospital. When he had entered the small private wing, a glance had confirmed his worst fears—but he had been forced to postpone a detailed examination. A blood transfusion was in progress: it was the second that day, according to Dr. Chai Vong, the *médecin indo-chinois* who was in charge in the absence of Dr. Chan Thornton. . . . With patent veins at a premium (as they always were in the gravely ill), there was no question of moving the sick man, even to apply the diaphragm of a stethoscope.

Inconclusive as the visit was, John had hardly needed Dr. Vong's report to confirm his own worst fears. He had left the room, where death hovered like a visible presence, without even pausing to ask for news of Chan: in a way, he was relieved that he must postpone a definite evaluation of his case.

Indra was waiting in the clinic hall when John left his patient's bedside. He saw she had changed from her coveralls to a white uniform with a stiffly starched bib: it was the badge of Johns Hopkins Nursing School graduates the world over.

"Chan had to go into the hills," she said. "He left a note to say he'll join us for dinner, at the latest. Could you examine our patient?"

"Not until the transfusion is finished. Dr. Vong is giving me a half-hour to unpack."

"The houseboys put your luggage in your old room beside the dispensary. When you're ready, I'll take you through Chan's lab."

"I'll look forward to that—after I've had a real look at Papa Oscar."

John found his quarters unchanged, down to the faded lithograph of King Thebaw, the twist of mosquito netting above the Spartan cot. The loose-leaf scrapbook, open on the bedside table, was the only added item: he guessed at once that Indra had placed it there. Each page was filled with clippings. Five years ago (on his last visit to Muong Toa), Oscar Thornton himself had exhibited those entries. It was the record of John's career—a glance told him that the practice had been continued. . . .

A murmur of voices outside the window distracted his attention briefly. Across the sunbaked rectangle of the hospital court, Dr. Vong was mounting the hospital steps with the journalist beside him. Wilde was talking breezily: when Vong paused with an arm stretched across the clinic door, John found himself smiling at the tableau. Obviously the spunky native doctor had just refused access to Oscar Thornton's bedside.

At this odd, relaxed moment, so different from the home-coming he had imagined, it was good to realize Lex Wilde would be held in bounds—and that he would occupy a room in the guesthouse, a safe distance from the compound. Thinking of the journalist, John's eyes were drawn again to the scrapbook. . . . When he had turned to its final paste-up, there was no need to wonder why Indra had left it for his inspection.

The page was filled with a single news story from the Paris edition of the New York *Times*—a digest of a paper John had given last fall, in Rome, before the International Congress of Microbiology. Most of it was an extended quote:

"The use of algal cultures for the production of food presents certain problems common to almost all the species studied," Dr. Merchant told the Congress, many of whose members have been experimenting with these microscopic bodies.

"Being one-celled organisms, algae are naturally delicate in character. They respond quickly to various stimuli, both beneficial and noxious. It is not true, as some laymen assume, that they are able to turn such unlimited raw materials as sunlight, carbon dioxide and water directly into food through the process known as photosynthesis. Algae are living beings. As such, they require special materials—minerals particularly—to bring this process to a workable conclusion.

"Photosynthesis, as we understand it, is the way plants grow. It involves the ability of chlorophyll to act as a catalyst and speed the basic chemical changes accompanying growth. Algae contain chlorophyll, just as the leaves of higher species. They repeat the same growth cycle. They can be harvested—in the true sense of the word—and used for food.

"Because of the delicacy of algae, they do not develop best in bright sunlight. The same is true of high temperature. Cooling and stirring are major problems wherever artificial growth stimulation is attempted.

"Some years ago, this problem and many others were

partially solved—at laboratory level—in Cambridge, Massachusetts. In carefully staged experiments, algal cultures were pumped through a series of plastic tubes, under direct sunlight. The method produced highly nutritious food material, satisfactory for human consumption. The process seemed most efficient when a particular species of algae, called *Chlorella pyrenoidosa,* was used.

"Unfortunately the Cambridge experiment showed that the cheapest harvest of edible nourishment obtained by this method would cost between twenty-five and fifty cents per pound. This fact alone ruled out its use as an ordinary nutrient. Most grains, particularly rice, can be grown much more cheaply.

"This year, in my own San Francisco laboratory," Dr. Merchant concluded, "I have devoted seven months to a similar process, in an effort to push this 'food factory' a few steps farther. My agent was a subspecies of algae which I had just succeeded in isolating; I had named it *Chlorella Thorntoni,* in honor of Dr. Oscar Thornton, the Nobel Prize winner and mentor of my youth.

"My findings will be reported in detail in the December Bulletin of the International Experiment Station, which joined with the Nutrition Foundation to make my experiments possible.

"At this time, I will say that the growth-rate of my subspecies indicates that its possibilities are considerable. Under the conditions of solar conversion described above, it has proved that its full-grown cells offer a harvest-blend of carbohydrates, proteins and fats more abundantly, and at a much lower cost, than existing species.

"This is easily the most promising breakthrough in the field of food production yet made in any experiment-series using algae."

As convention papers went, John reflected, the facts in the *Times* dispatch were sobersided enough—until those final paragraphs. At the time of its delivery, he could hardly believe the average newspaper reader (panting for rumors of

10

Armageddon and high-life scandal) would stay with his discourse to the end. The response, when it came, had been startling. His current backer, the Nutrition Foundation, had received an avalanche of mail: the detailed breakdown of the process, as reported in the Station *Bulletin*, had brought a spate of queries from scientists at home and abroad.

Chan Thornton had not been among those correspondents. Chan had broken a five-year silence with the radiogram summoning John to his father's bedside.

The microbiologist had fully understood his friend's silence: he was sure that Chan (like other researchers, all over the world) was involved in similar experiments. The scrapbook beside his bed was proof that his judgment had been accurate: he could afford a quiet chuckle at Chan's rather obvious reminder. . . . The nature of the younger Thornton's work would be revealed shortly, John was sure: if there had been progress, the results would be exhibited with the flourish that was Chan's hallmark. Meanwhile, his friend was enjoying a favorite gambit, the creation of a mystery. It was even possible his absence that afternoon was deliberate.

John's mind, released from a yearlong treadmill of trial and error that is the lot of all research biologists, refused to grapple with Chan's motives. Instead, he pushed up the tall screen on his window and stepped out to the balcony to savor the ageless scene more fully.

The wind that had delayed their landing had fallen to a whisper, now the day was ending. It was strong enough to bring the fragrance of Chin-ling's garden.

The massed blooms and hedges, rising in tiers on the hill behind the director's residence, had been the first sight to greet John Merchant's eyes when he had arrived here (with no companion but an amah) to become Dr. Oscar Thornton's ward. At that time, some twenty years in the past, the doctor's Mandarin wife had long been dead: John's only image of her was the painting that hung in the study. . . . Then as now, Chin-ling's monuments had been that same garden, and the son she had given Oscar Thornton. It had always seemed fitting to John that boxwood dragons and Tartar horsemen

11

should mingle with those banks of English roses and camellias —just as Chan, in his own person, had combined the best qualities of East and West.

John had been only nine when he entered this compound for the first time—to stare in wonder at the immaculate white walls of the hospital and the screened porches of the mission school. He could still see the boy's figure clearly, recall his frantic heartbeat when he opened the door of the director's office for the interview that would change his life.

Oscar Thornton had been a towering figure that morning— a man of forty whose ample private means (joined to a grant from a mission board) had made Muong Toa's abundance possible. On the day of John's arrival in the clinic office, Dr. Thornton had come direct from his operating room: a surgeon's mask still hung at his neck when he took the boy's hand in both his own.

"We hoped you'd arrive sooner, John."

"I couldn't arrange transport from Delhi, sir."

"At least you knew your home was ready. I think you'll like it here. It's a good place to grow."

The tears had come then, though the boy had fought to hold them back. His parents, medical missionaries in South India, had died within days of one another, in the backwash of a cholera epidemic, while John was at school in Simla. Save for the fact that Dr. Thornton and the Reverend Peter Merchant had once been college classmates, he would have had nowhere to turn.

"Time heals most wounds, including the loss you've just endured," said the hospital director. "We'll do our best to make you happy."

"I can look after myself, Dr. Thornton."

"The details were settled years ago, John. For the present, you can pick up your schooling here. We'll give you full instruction through the grammar grades. Afterwards, you must leave the Valley: you and Chan will be sent out together. Is it too soon to ask what you intend to be?"

"I'm going to be a doctor." It was the first time the boy had put his dream into words. Once it was uttered, he could feel the tears dry on his cheek.

"So is my son," said Oscar Thornton. "You aren't saying this to flatter me?"

"I don't know how to flatter, sir."

"Nor do I, John. We'll bring up the subject later—after you've settled in here. Don't think I'll be hurt if you decide to be a movie star. Or a Texas oilman."

"I won't change."

"It's only instinct speaking, but I'm sure you won't. If I'm right, you've discovered Fray Luis de Leon's formula for happiness at an early age."

"Who was he?"

"One of the Spanish mystics. *'The beauty of life,'* he said, *'is no more than this—that each man should act in conformity with his nature and his business.' "*

"Is *this* the business you've always wanted?"

"From the beginning," said Oscar Thornton. "Fortunately, I had two of those Texas oilmen for grandfathers, so I could gratify my desire. What's more, I've made it possible for Chan to follow in my footsteps, if he's so inclined. Perhaps, like you, he'll end by demanding a wider horizon."

"Why can't we both work here—at your hospital?"

"Chan will succeed me, I hope: half his heritage is Oriental, so it's logical for him to remain. When the time is right, you'll return to your own people—unless you decide to be a citizen of the world. They're still a rare breed, John: we produce them occasionally. I'm raising one now in the mission school. Another of my wards—a girl a little younger than you named Indra Lal. A Khmer. Do you know the Khmer, by any chance?"

"I'm afraid not, Doctor."

"They were a noble people once. Angkor Wat, in Cambodia, is their handiwork. Indra is a direct descendant of Queen Indradevi, the wife of the great Jayavarman. I have books to prove it." The hospital director smiled at John's bewildered look. "Don't think I'm dazzled by blue blood—it's still a fact in anthropology. Indra was only a teacher's daughter when I took her in, but I'm willing to gamble on her future. Someday she'll head my nursing school. She may even marry Chan. Or you—if you find East and West can really meet."

"Can they, sir?"

Oscar Thornton glanced at the painting on the wall, a full-length portrait of a woman in a golden gown. Her dark hair was caught in ivory pins; her smile distilled a radiance that warmed the newcomer instantly. John needed a moment to realize this was the doctor's dead wife.

"*I've* shown they could meet," said Oscar Thornton. "It was the greatest discovery I ever made."

The interview (brief though it was) had been an overture to an existence that could only be called ideal, to a span of years that had changed a boy into a man.

The hours John spent in the open-air classrooms of the mission school had passed swiftly. When books were closed for the day, he had roamed the Valley at will—with Chan Thornton at his side, and Indra Lal a frequent companion. They had hunted and fished in mountain gorges, climbed trails that led to the monastery gates and the upland meadows, explored the caves that honeycombed the bases of the Gates of Hell. On holidays, they had slept in Meo huts or bivouacked under the stars. . . . Indra, to her intense disgust, had been excluded from the camping. Otherwise, she had been treated as an equal—especially after the boys discovered she could outclimb them and was the best shot of the three.

The curriculum had ended at the mission long before John wished to leave Muong Toa—and, as Oscar Thornton had promised, the three had been sent to the United States for further training. Indra had graduated from the Johns Hopkins School of Nursing and Radcliffe, with a degree she would need as a teacher in the field. Chan and John had taken their own medical degrees at Hopkins—where they had found their major interest lay in the field of microbiology, a speciality that had burgeoned during the war. They had completed their graduate studies at Harvard, on a schedule that kept the threesome unbroken.

During those student years—whether he wore the uniform of the ROTC or a laboratory coat—Chan Thornton had been

14

a strikingly handsome youth, a prince from Cathay whose future was bounded by special horizons. John (whose own horizon was contained in a microscope) had been glad they had chosen the same medical field. When the younger Thornton had returned to his father's hospital like a dutiful son, John could understand the choice. The family wells in Texas continued to spout black gold: Chan's father had already promised to back his ambitious plans for research in tropical medicine.

A year later, Indra had left America to head Papa Oscar's nursing school, and to assist in his busy outpatient clinic. There had been times in that last year when John had been almost sure she would make a different choice: when he had discovered his first fellowship grant would support a wife, he had even asked her to remain. . . . He had found no argument to combat her refusal. Loyalty to Oscar Thornton had made her return to Muong Toa inevitable.

Two years after her departure, young Dr. Merchant had chalked up his first triumph—the discovery of a new antibiotic which had controlled an exploding epidemic of typhoid in the Philippines. After he had correlated his findings in Manila, and submitted to photographers and interviews, he had obeyed a compulsive need and flown direct to the Enchanted Valley.

The elder Thornton, he found, had turned silver gray, but his vigor seemed undiminished when they sat down in the consulting room where they had first met.

"Well, John? Did I guess right, about all of you?"

"It wasn't guesswork in my case, sir."

"I've followed the literature of your specialities: I've kept a newspaper file of your achievement. There's no need to ask if you're happy in your calling."

"Not too happy to transfer here, if I can be useful."

"I've both my son and Indra as helpers now."

"Surely Muong Toa can use an extra medical man."

"So can any hospital. You've moved far beyond medicine since we last met."

"You've given Chan one of the finest labs I've ever seen. We could do tropical research together."

"At Hopkins, you were friendly rivals. The rivalry continued at Cambridge. Could you keep your friendship green if you settled in my valley?"

"Why not?"

"For one thing, you asked Indra to stay in America."

"Did she tell you that?"

"Indra has always confided in me. She was strongly tempted to accept your offer. In the end, she put duty before desire."

"She could hardly do less, sir. Neither can I—if I'm needed here."

"Your work lies beyond this valley, John, in a far larger world. You've fulfilled my hopes in that world. What foster-father could ask for more?"

"Are you satisfied with progress here?"

"While I'm alive, Muong Toa will prosper. Afterwards, the responsibility will be Chan's. Perhaps our mountain enclave will go on forever as it does today. Indra's become a first-rate manager. Chan is a scientist of the highest ability—"

"What of the threat to the north?"

"So far, Peiping has been too concerned with its survival to trouble us."

"I'm told it's a miracle you've kept your freedom."

"Put that down to luck, John—and geography. Nothing has changed here. I pray that nothing will."

"Your enemies tell a different story."

"American newspapers are flown in to us regularly—so I've heard those voices too. Most of the pundits are sure I've joined forces with the Communists. Or at least approved their take-over in China."

"I've never believed that, sir," John said quickly.

"Of course you haven't. You know what I've tried to accomplish here. When I came to this country thirty years ago, most of its inhabitants were living in the Bronze Age. I was a green young doctor—positive that medical skill and good intentions could solve everything. I won't say I've brought about a millennium. I *have* taught the people of this valley to live in peace. They've taught me more about the essential dignity of man than I could ever hope to learn elsewhere."

"No wonder you've been happy here."

"I've had a rewarding life, John. So have my people. They've prospered, according to their standards, and they've been content to stay within their horizon. If the Gates of Hell aren't breached, they'll keep those virtues intact."

"Chan could have written his own ticket in the States. Has he had second thoughts about returning?"

"Chan is a natural-born scientist, with an urge to blaze new trails in tropical medicine. He's had an ideal proving ground in Muong Toa."

"Can he continue to do research—and take your place?"

"Easily, with Indra as his balance wheel. He'll hit his stride before I die. I'll admit he's yet to learn the tricks of the successful administrator. Sometimes, he's impatient with the slow minds around him—"

The elder Thornton, John perceived, was that rarest of mortals, a parent who saw the limitations of his offspring as well as their strength. It was true that Chan Thornton was the quintessence of both East and West. There had always been arrogance beneath the brilliance, a driving need to excel, a towering ego that had made enemies in his university years.

"A doctor like Chan needs more than a single outlet," said Oscar Thornton. "I was content to be a healer—to add a few footnotes to the story of man's rise from savagery. My son has more ambitious dreams. *He'll* never rest—until he has written a formula to save the world."

Hearing the echoes of that last meeting (as clearly as though he had just left the man's presence), John Merchant stepped down from his bedroom balcony and approached the west wing of the hospital.

A wide sweep of lawn separated the compound from the director's residence, and the guesthouse that adjoined it. Chan Thornton's dwelling was connected with the clinic by a stone pergola, heavy with flowering bougainvillea. There was a bench near the end of this green tunnel. Five years ago, John had sat there with Indra Lal beside him, watching the dance of fireflies in the vines while they discussed his future and her own.

"It's always a risk, returning to a place where you passed

your childhood," she had told him. "Are you sorry you came back?"

"You took that risk. Why shouldn't I?"

"I belong here, John."

"Don't pretend you didn't love your years in Baltimore and Cambridge."

"I did love them, but they're behind me now."

"I'll admit the Valley has its special charm. Papa Oscar and Chin-ling saw to that. Can it ever mean as much to you?"

"Why not—if Chan and I find ways to make the enchantment last?"

"That's his job now. It isn't necessarily yours. I needn't tell you how I feel about you, Indra. It's been plain as day from the beginning."

She did not answer—and when he cupped her chin in his palm, he saw her eyes were brimming with tears.

"This isn't our sort of game, John," she said. "We'll be sorry we played it tomorrow."

"I'm not playing a game. I'm asking you to come back to America—as my wife. What's wrong with that?"

The tears were gone when she turned to face him. There was resolution in her eyes, a glow of courage he had seen there often—and loved, until tonight. For a moment, they looked at each other without speaking. When she leaned forward and kissed him gently, he knew she had given him her answer—but not the one he had wanted.

"Does Chan need you that much?"

"He will—after his father's too old to keep the reins."

"Perhaps I should stay."

"You can't—for more than one reason. Even now, Chan gives nearly all his time to the laboratory—"

"We could work there together."

"Would you take that risk?"

"What risk is involved? We're both research biologists."

"He's good at his work—but you're even better. If there's one thing Chan Thornton won't accept, it's second place. We must let him go on alone. It's best for us all."

She rose to go—but he continued to hold her hands as they

18

stood close together in the warm darkness. "*I'm* the one who'll be alone, Indra. Chan will have you."

"You're strong enough in yourself, John. You don't need anyone else." Her voice broke on the words. Suddenly she was in his arms, kissing him with a wild passion he'd never dared to hope for. It was only a brief surrender. Before he could claim her lips again, she had vanished in the leafy tunnel.

"*C'est vous, monsieur le docteur?*"

John rose from his reverie. Dr. Chai Vong had appeared at the clinic door, to peer doubtfully into the shadow-pattern of the pergola.

"Has he wakened?"

"The transfusion produced no change. You may examine him now, if you wish."

The microbiologist had dismissed his private vision before he mounted the hospital porch. One truth was self-evident. Five years had elapsed since that tortured parting—but Indra Lal, for all the unstinting help she had given Chan and Oscar Thornton, had kept her own name and her own counsel.

In the hall that divided the men's ward, John glanced briefly into each of the long, airy rooms. Less than half the beds were occupied, a detail that spoke well for Indra's stewardship. At Muong Toa, spring was a season when the endemic patterns of most diseases reached their peak.

Two other facts registered on the visitor's mind. Only here and there did he observe the dark-featured Meo and Kha tribesmen who made up the usual backlog of patients. Most of the bed cases were lighter-skinned Lao; at least a dozen were Chinese. He was more surprised to note that nearly all the obvious injuries involved broken limbs, encased in casts or suspended in traction frames. In that bemused moment, he found neither fact too startling. Broken bones had been no novelty in the ward during his last visit, when the villagers were finishing the masonwork on their irrigation dam. The men's ward had always been polyglot: the Valley was open to all settlers, regardless of their origin.

Dr. Vong opened the door to the private wing, and the room where the hospital director lay. Indra was waiting at the foot of the elevated bed with the patient's chart in her hand. John scanned the telltale notations quickly. Since the patient was in coma, he made no attempt to cover his first reaction.

"Didn't the transfusion help at all?"

"*Un peu*, Dr. Merchant," said Vong, in the same lisping French. "They cannot postpone collapse. As you see, I have noted the hemorrhages from the mucous membranes. Despite the fresh blood, he is again almost exsanguinated."

The waxen figure on the bed was barely clinging to life. In his prime, Oscar Thornton had been muscled like a latter-day Hercules. Today, he was less than an effigy of his former self. The still-handsome profile resembled one of those death masks that suggest each bone in the skull, beneath drum-tight skin. When John lifted a wrist, the pulse was hurried and thready: the easy compression of the artery was a sure sign of dangerously low pressure, as was the shallow respiration.

The distention of the left upper abdomen completed the classic pattern of the disease that cut into Oscar Thornton's last productive years. In Muong Toa, an enlarged spleen had once indicated malaria, but the disease had been almost eradicated in the Valley. One other prediction remained, and John refused to voice it. . . . No obvious treatment was indicated. Extra transfusions might improve the blood pressure, shortening the clotting time and controlling those lethal hemorrhages. The medications from San Francisco (all of them Draconian, last-ditch measures) might postpone the inevitable. The visiting doctor could do no more than prolong his patient's tenure.

"Is there any hope from chemotherapy?" Vong asked.

"I can't say until I've seen a blood-smear."

Indra spoke, for the first time. "I have slides waiting."

"We'll keep up the transfusions, so long as we can find a a vein."

"He's type O," said Indra. "You can match him easily."

"I remember how often he gave blood to patients. Can you find donors?"

"The Valley will open its veins," said the *médecin indochinois*.

"When did you first note the abdominal swelling?"

"Almost six months ago. *Le père* Oscar made his own diagnosis." Vong's eyes brushed past Indra, and his lips formed the French word for leukemia. "Until the transfer of authority to Dr. Chan, he held death at arm's length. Now, as you see, the hemorrhages have changed the picture drastically."

John put down the chart and turned to Indra. "Why wasn't I sent for earlier?"

"I begged him to ask you to come. So did Chan. He said he was ready to die."

"But you did send word, after he'd lapsed into coma?"

He saw her wince at the accusation in his tone. "Chan knew you would take the first plane, no matter how slim the chances were."

"This is the only time I've sided with son against father," John said quietly. "I'll check those slides now."

The hospital's clinical laboratory was a department in its own right, distinct from Chan Thornton's domain. When Indra led John to the specimen table, the room was empty. The miscroscope, he noted, was a modern binocular. The display of reagents and culture tubes gleamed with newness.

"You'll find a slide on the stage," said Indra. She had paused in the doorway, with folded arms; once again, John felt a mounting frustration at her refusal to open her mind.

Pulling a stool close to the microscope, he saw that the exhibit under the lenses was touched with the reddish hue of the standard gram stain. When he brought the blood-smear into focus, he found the slide loaded with round cells of various sizes. Each had its own dark nucleus and its rim of cytoplasm. There was only a scattering of normal lympho-cytic bodies in the group. By far the larger number exhibited an oddly-shaped mitotic pattern in the nuclei. It was characteristic of the malignant blood-condition (literally cancer) known as leukemia.

"Dr. Vong whispered the word," John said. "Shall I speak it aloud?"

"Please do," Indra had advanced a step into the room. He could sense that she was groping for a personal note, however tentative.

"Obviously, it's an advanced case of lymphatic leukemia. The hemorrhages suggest it's in a terminal phase."

"Could you have saved him, if you'd had the case earlier?"

"There's no known cure, of course. The drugs I've brought might have kept him alive another half-year or so. As things stand now, he'll be gone in a matter of days."

"Will you let him go?"

John lifted his eyes from the lenses. He would have accepted the query from Dr. Vong: life, in the Eastern mind, was a weed that could be valued lightly. He had expected another view from the descendant of a Khmer king.

"When I left San Francisco," he said, "I told my assistant to stand by for orders. He's ready to fly here at once, with any supplies I request. Meanwhile, I'm keeping Papa Oscar alive by any means at hand. Some of us in the field have hoped we were on the brink of a cancer cure. What if the discovery came tomorrow?"

Indra flushed. It was the first time he had breached the wall of her reserve.

"I'm sorry, John. It's only that he was ready for death. I had no right to echo his despair."

"It's hard to picture Oscar Thornton in despair."

The girl shrugged, but did not pursue the topic. "What medication did you bring?"

"I've a week's supply of all the antileukemic drugs. Nitrogen mustard's ruled out, I'm afraid: he's much too frail to stand the side effects. We've had some good results with Six-MP—Six-mercaptopurine in the *materia medica*."

"Can you start it now?"

"I'd rather wait a few hours—until we can be sure there's no transfusion reaction."

Perhaps it was the knowledge they had done what could be done for the dying man, but Indra seemed to unbend when she opened the side door that gave to the compound. They paused on the stoop to watch the sunset burn the crest of Butterfly Mountain, a green eminence that filled the eastern sky beyond the Gates of Hell. The fading light gave the nearby village the air of a Japanese print, and painted the

22

surface of the irrigation lake a dove gray: it was a time of day John had always loved.

"I'll radio Dudley Porter to join us," he said, "after he's checked the latest findings at the National Research Institute. Are you ready to take me through Chan's lab—or is that his sole province?"

Indra's eyes were on the distant mountain. Below the monastery gate, a great puff of swallows had erupted from a ledge, to whirl in the sun's last rays before they settled. The phenomenon belonged to day's end in Muong Toa. As a boy, John had half-believed the mountain had sent forth a cryptic message only the Buddhist monks could read.

"Chan and I have worked together for eight years," the girl said. "I've given him every moment I could spare from the hospital. Laboratory technique was part of my training at Hopkins."

"In that case, you'll be a proper guide," he said. "I hope I'm worthy of the honor." Following Indra to the low-eaved building across the compound, John hoped the words had covered a sudden stab of pain. Somehow, he had expected Chan Thornton to work at lone-wolf level: he had never pictured Indra as a fellow researcher.

"You'll find we've used our time well," she said.

"If you prefer, we can wait for his return."

Intent on selecting a key from a ring in the pocket of her uniform, Indra turned back from the door. Her smile was an enigma he would ponder later.

"Have you forgotten Chan's note? He directed me to show you the lab, the moment you'd finished with Papa Oscar."

"How often must I insist I'm an eager tourist?"

"You'll be more than a tourist in a moment," said the girl, and fitted her key to the lock.

The laboratory had double doors, with a vestibule between. Both portals had heavy padlocks, equipped with steel bars. Together with the iron-shuttered windows and the heavy slate roof, they gave Chan's sanctum the air of an aboveground vault jealous of its treasures. When Indra had lifted the last bar, John saw her cicerone's pride was warranted. Five years ago, his friend's workroom had been a simple shed, open to the air and sun. He was unprepared for this vista of zinc worktables, the shining pyramids of glass and steel, the purr of air conditioners—though Muong Toa had always boasted its own electric plant.

"Why the Fort Knox atmosphere?" he asked. "Are you guarding the philosopher's stone—or the secret of perpetual motion?"

"Not quite," said Indra. "We find it's simpler to keep this building locked. There's a fortune in antibiotics on those shelves. To say nothing of the colorimeters and our electron microscope. You can imagine what this equipment has cost the Thornton Trust."

"Don't tell me you have thieves in Eden?"

"We've tried hard to banish robbers from our midst. We can hardly control the average man's curiosity."

"Are you thinking of my distinguished fellow traveler?"

Indra Lal touched a light switch. "Mr. Wilde is no problem this afternoon. I've sent him on a tour of the Valley in our second Land Rover, with a houseboy at the wheel." She continued to move about the long, low-ceilinged room, lighting neon-clusters above the tables. "Even if he could grasp what I'm about to show you, we're not ready for *his* brand of reporting."

"I'll agree with that unreservedly."

"Just to be doubly sure, I'll lock us in before we start your tour."

Standing aside to let the girl pass down the center aisle of the main workroom, John continued to stare at the new equipment the neons had revealed. He did not risk a comment until Indra returned from the vestibule.

"Obviously no expense has been spared to give Chan what he needed."

"You saw that much on your last visit."

"He must have ten times the facilities today." The microbiologist moved toward the first worktable, letting his hand rest on a high-speed centrifuge: the gesture—like the handclasp of an old friend—helped to restore his sense of proportion. The next table, he saw, was equipped for the biochemical tests necessary to evaluate the amino acid content

24

of any given protein sample. The one beyond bristled with the complex tools of microchemistry.

"Most of the work done here is routine," said Indra. "As you see, we're making a specialty of food-processing."

"Papa Oscar was never satisfied with the yield from his farms."

"Nor are we, John." She moved on to another table. "These plastic blocks are used to test the life cycles of algae. We'll come back to them later."

"What's in the room beyond?"

"Two major experiments—a mice-run to retest the jungle typhus virus Chan isolated a year ago, and a setup for culturing leukemia cells. Papa Oscar ordered that one just after he was stricken."

John nodded soberly. It was like Oscar Thornton to insist that the agent causing his own death be used as a possible instrument of healing.

"Have you had any luck?"

"None so far. You're familiar with the isolation of the jungle typhus virus, aren't you?"

"I read Chan's report. With a virus as the proved cause, they can't call it typhus any more." John paused at the mice-run, to look down at the scurrying shadows of a dozen rodents, stimulated to activity by the light. "May I see your leukemia setup?"

Indra led the way round a bank of incubators—all of them filled with racked culture tubes. Nearby, on a wide table, John noted a file of microscopes; beyond, a pair of cables led to an X-ray machine. In one corner, a small computer suggested that physics, rather than chemistry, was on review there.

"This hardly seems an abandoned project," he said.

"Chan promised his father to keep hammering at the problem. As you see, we're keeping a close check on results—or rather, the lack of them."

"What's the present approach?"

"For the past month, we've been tabulating fundamental changes in cell proteins."

"Using leukemia cultures?"

"Only as background, to establish the malignancy. Chan's made over a hundred comparisons with normal tissue—after we'd exposed it to X ray for possible mutation."

"A project of this size takes personnel. Where do you get your help?"

"Four technicians work here every day. We have three more lined up as apprentices. All of them are graduates of the mission school. Chan and I trained them between us."

"I knew research was his ruling passion, Indra. But I never thought he'd train others. Chan wasn't cut out to be a teacher."

"He was meant for this work—just as you were. I'm the administrator. If you must know, I did most of that training."

Indra had retraced her path among the plywood sides of the mice-run. In the main room, she led John among the worktables until they reached the eastern wall of the laboratory, where a pair of sliding panels (fitted with bars and padlocks, like the outer doors) shut off a second alcove from view. Here the girl slipped a key into the new padlock, then hesitated for an instant, for no reason John could grasp.

"Shall I step back?" he asked. "Will it leap out at me—like a jack-in-the-box?"

Indra's shoulders stiffened, but she made no attempt to match his feeble wit. Instead, she bent to turn the key, lifted the steel bar, and pushed the panels wide.

The double doors, moving on well-oiled casters, slid into their containing walls without sound.

The alcove was darkened, but the dying day—filtered through a skylight that sloped almost to ground level—outlined a worktable just inside the portals. Beyond it was a squat object that resembled, at first glance, a squid blown to nightmare size. The comparison was enhanced by a score of pale-white tentacles, writhing slowly beneath the skylight. These outsized plastic tubes, John observed, extended into a walled courtyard, where they could receive further exposure to sunlight, yet remain concealed from prying eyes.

To one side was a concrete-walled pool, connected to the squidlike body by metal pipes. Its function, John knew, was to insure a constant supply of fluids—the monster's life, and its excuse for being. . . . Indra had already moved into the alcove to touch a wall switch. The room sprang into brilliance, changing the giant squid to what it was—a solar convertor, similar to the model John had built in his San Francisco workroom.

Despite its size, he needed only a glance to know this was a near-replica of the glass-and-metal complex he had designed for his own work in algal culture. Like the centrifuge in the outer lab, he could accept it as a friend who had helped him —and, on occasion, exasperated him beyond measure. He was hardly surprised to find it here: a model of the apparatus had been sketched, in detail, in the same issue of the Station *Bulletin* that had described his isolation of *Chlorella Thorntoni*.

Indra had already stood aside to give John free access to the alcove. He found he was circling the huge machine without speaking, to check (and admire) the details of Chan Thornton's handiwork. The heart of the monster was its metal body, and the powerful pump that circulated the various cultures of algae it processed. Beside it was a settling chamber, where the harvesting of the so-called algal "crop" was accomplished, after the growth cycle had ended in those plastic tubes.

Basically, John saw that Chan was prepared to follow the procedure he had laid down in the *Bulletin*. While the pump was in action, a constant, slow-moving mixture (composed of water, masses of algae, and a nutrient medium) was exposed to the sun's rays via the thin-walled plastic tubes. It was here that the culture, and the chlorophyll it contained, used solar energy to perform its function—the physicochemical conversion of water, carbon dioxide and nutrient into full-grown cells.

In the court, a steel pipe connected the convertor with a furnace producing $CO_2$ (the chemist's shortcut term for carbon dioxide), a gas as essential to algal growth as breath to the human body. Another pipe charged the apparatus with the carefully balanced nutrient, from a vat whose contents were replenished at the will of the operator. By varying the charge, John knew, a single technician could fix the percentages of proteins, carbohydrates and fat in each adult cell with surprising accuracy. Depending on the efficiency of the monster (and the solar stimulation that was its governor), he could also estimate the daily yield to within a few kilograms.

John spoke at last, with both hands on the convertor (a spelling he had used in his original paper, to emphasize the function of the machine).

"Chan has done a magnificent job."

"He was always a genius with tools." Indra, he saw, had accepted his praise eagerly. He could only guess at the part she had played in this patient reconstruction of his model.

"Wasn't it difficult to get materials?"

"Not with the Thornton Trust behind us. Chan felt sure the results would justify the investment."

"It's far ahead of any convertor I've inspected. It should have a special name."

"Our technicians call it a *bat jhow yee.*"

John searched his memory for Chinese pidgin. "Eight-legged fish?"

"Literally an octopus," said Indra. "As you see, this one has many extra arms. Don't use the name in Chan's presence, please. A sense of humor isn't among his virtues."

She touched a switch, activating a motor deep in the monster's body and setting the main pump in motion. In a short time, the patternless writhing of the coils changed to a steady pulsation, as the pump gave a rhythmic impetus to their contents. While John watched, a valve clicked—actuated by a solenoid switch—and a charge of the watery medium in which the algae grew, distending each tube as it completed the circuit, brought the *bat jhow yee* to vibrant life.

"Waste from the whole Valley is brought in each morning," said Indra. "On clear days, we manage to convert most of it to edible calories. The excess is burned off in the furnace outside."

"I take it there are no aesthetic objections."

"The Oriental mind has never been troubled by such Western prejudices. Besides, the whole process is hidden by that
28

wall outside. The villagers can't do more than guess at what we're accomplishing."

"What about your technicians?"

"They help only with details. They couldn't begin to grasp our purpose."

"Will you review the procedure—to make sure *I* can follow it?"

Indra rose coolly to the challenge: a slight flush told him she had been stirred by the implied compliment to her knowledge.

"I needn't tell you we've broken no new ground here, so far. All Chan has really done is expand current models and speed up their performance." She disengaged the pump as she spoke: it continued to throb a moment more, then rumbled into silence.

"The solar exposure is especially ingenious. I see that he's added a light-density meter."

"It operates a rheostat, governing the speed of the circulation."

John nodded. Even now, when each detail seemed engraved on his brain, he could not take his eyes away. Controlled by the light meter, the convertor pump would operate more rapidly in bright sunlight—to keep the temperature of the culture medium from rising too high. The rate would slow on cloudy days, insuring each algal cell its quota of light, regardless of weather.

"Climatic conditions must be ideal here," he said.

"Muong Toa has more days of sunshine than most of southeast Asia. We've checked our growth-rate against yours. Our *bat jhow yee* tops the best convertors in America: the figures are almost twice as high."

"I'll accept that conclusion. Just how is it charged?"

"The growth medium feeds in here; the second pipe forces in carbon dioxide from the opposite side. The circuit ends in the settling chamber. By that time, the new, full-grown cells are heavy enough to fall to the bottom. We harvest them on porcelain filters that drain off the liquid and return it to the culture vat. The filters have a drying-tray that goes

29

straight to the furnace. Each evening, we weigh the day's yield and store it. If we wished, it could be used as food tomorrow."

"Nothing's wasted, then—including the original charge."

"Chan's particularly proud of that detail."

"Could I see this yield you spoke of?"

Indra moved to the head of the worktable, where a metric scale was mounted beside a rack of numbered weighing-trays. John noted that each container held several kilograms of granular powder. Most of the powder was of a greenish hue.

"One of the difficulties with algae," Indra said, "is to make the end product palatable. We've experimented with various condiments and settled on the fish sauce they mix with rice in Muong Toa." She took a measuring spoon from a drawer, scooped up a small portion of the powder, and offered it to the microbiologist. "Will you sample our elixir, Doctor?"

"Food from the sun, and the earth's heart?"

"Is the concept too fanciful?"

"Of course not. Those are pure calories in that spoon. There's no better nourishment anywhere. I've made it myself —but never in this quantity."

As he spoke, John took the spoon from Indra, conquered an instinctive grimace, and swallowed the contents. The taste was an exact match for the standard fish-and-rice diet he had eaten in his travels among primitive peoples. The sauce, blended with the powder, had canceled out the slightly brown taste of the algae.

"What's your cost per kilo?"

"Just under fifty cents."

"That beats our own rate of twenty-five cents a pound."

"Cost is still the great stumbling block." For an instant, he thought Indra would say more. Then, with an air of a patient guide who has completed a scheduled tour (and is eager to close the museum doors) she moved toward the panels that opened to the main laboratory. "If you'll come this way, we'll look at our test units. Chan's proud of them too."

The testing table (which Indra had dismissed with a few words during their inspection of the larger room) was a familiar universe to John—a reproduction in miniature of the functions he had just observed in the solar convertor.

Here, of course, the reproduction of the algal life cycle was far simpler. High-voltage bulbs were reflected by mirrors through a series of plastic blocks, each of which was hollowed to form a double chamber. Water was circulated through the outer hollow to keep the inner chamber cool. In the blocks, algae could be developed under constant observation, stimulated by precisely regulated amounts of culture medium and carbon dioxide. Both agents were injected into each block through glass pipettes. At the base of each inner chamber, a third pipette collected full-grown cells as they settled.

"Dudley Porter would be in his element here," John said.

"Is he your chief assistant?"

"My man Friday—and a wizard at this kind of harvesting."

"Chan would welcome him, I'm sure. Our own technicians aren't too expert."

John had already paused at the last of the plastic blocks, to study the culture medium carefully. "Do you have a current report on this setup?"

"Of course. It's on that shelf. I'm glad you chose your own *Chlorella Thorntoni.*" Indra pointed to the rack that stood above the worktable. A series of clipboards contained the day's tabulations: the growth-rate of each culture, together with precise notes on the medium employed.

"Apparently you've had excellent results from this block."

"We have. You'll find a hanging-drop preparation on the worktable, if you'd like to see it under the scope."

The "hanging drop," John knew, was the name microbiologists gave to an ingenious method for studying growth-patterns, while the elements involved were still viable. A thick glass slide with a cuplike depression at its center was employed in this demonstration. Using the slide as a base, and a thin smear of vaseline as an anchor, a single drop of the culture was placed on a wafer-thin cover slip that was then pressed down above the cup. The vaseline sealed off the tiny chamber in which the exhibit now hung. When prepared by an expert hand, the hanging drop became, in essence, a miniature laboratory containing enough oxygen to keep the medium alive for extensive study. The advantages of such a technique were infinite. Perhaps the greatest was the fact that cell function could be observed under conditions almost identical with normal growth.

John peered down through the two eyepieces of the microscope Indra had just lighted and twirled the adjustment that brought the hanging drop into focus. Once again, he was looking down at a cosmos that had become even more familiar than his own. It seemed quite natural to rediscover it, eight thousand miles from his own workroom.

"It's really my subspecies, Indra. I'm glad it found its way here." The microbiologist cut off the light and removed the hanging drop from the stage. Indra's demonstration, it seemed, had ended with this item, but he could not help feeling it was merely a prologue.

"I'd like to see a rundown on performance," he said.

"The notes are in the wall cabinet. I'm afraid only Chan can explain them. They're partly in Chinese."

"Even in Cambridge, he thought in both languages. It drove his professors mad. Regardless of the language, I can see he's far ahead of my own findings."

"He'll like that."

"I'm sure he will. After all, we both know why he started growing algae."

Indra did not stir in the shadow beyond the droplight.

"Do you mean the old need to be first?"

"Wasn't that his original motive?"

"Do you blame him for trying to solve Asia's food problem in this room?"

"Of course not. I was drawn to algae growing for the same reason. In the West, my work's been stymied by aesthetic objections—mostly the use of waste as an essential raw material. Here there's no such impasse. That's why Chan's milieu is perfect."

Indra moved to the alcove, and the weighing-tray, to sift a handful of the greenish powder through her fingers. "When you sampled this product, could you tell it from the sticky rice you've eaten all over Asia?"

"The taste was identical." John chose his words, aware of the challenge behind the question. "We both know it's twenty times richer in protein. If we could produce it like rice, we could abolish hunger."

"Chan hopes to do just that."

"Abolish *hunger?*"

"He has a plan."

"The roadblock remains, Indra. How do we cut the cost?"

"I'll let Chan answer that."

John looked up sharply. Absorbed as he was, he had missed the click of a key in the lock of the outer door—but he had heard the rasp of the lifted crossbar. The portal swung open before he could join Indra in the aisle between the worktables. Darkness had already invaded the compound: the man on the threshold carried a bull's-eye lantern. Even in that goblin light John knew it was Chan Thornton.

Chan crossed the outer vestibule in two quick strides before he put down the lantern. John had already moved down the aisle, with a shouted greeting.

His mind had identified his friend instantly: his heart could half-believe this was Oscar Thornton in his heyday. Even as a youth, Chan had possessed his father's good looks, his abounding vitality. Today, at thirty, he had simply expanded to match the mold. There were already hints of gray in the younger Thornton's hair: the map of crow's-feet around his eyes was advertisement of his hours of toil in this room. Save for the slightly almond pattern of those eyes, there was no real trace of his Chinese mother. Chan, John reflected, could have belonged to any race or creed. When their hands joined, he felt the confusions of a long day dissolve. Oscar Thornton, it seemed, had passed on his heritage.

"We've been inspecting your handiwork, Chan. I hope you don't mind."

"You're here on my order, John. I wanted to save you time. I hope Indra's been an inspired guide."

"Isn't she always?"

"Tonight, she had good reason." Chan glanced toward the doors of the alcove, and the silhouette of the convertor. "I hope you'll forgive me for omitting this item in my radio-gram."

"You gave me reason enough for coming."

"Vong tells me you may be able to help Father a little—with Six-MP."

"It's worth a try. Shall we go back to the hospital, and see if he's ready?"

"Vong will call us, if we're needed."

John was briefly chilled by the dryness of his friend's tone. He had felt obscurely that some reunion at Papa Oscar's bed-side was called for, however futile it might be.

"You're right, of course, Chan. We can't risk a transfusion reaction now."

"In that case, I'd suggest we stay here a while longer—un-less you're too tired to go over my findings."

Echoing the younger Thornton's smile, as they faced each other across the worktable, John found that five years of ab-sence had vanished in that shared agreement. (This, after all, was the land of the living. Oscar Thornton would have been the first to insist that the workday at Muong Toa continue without hiatus.)

"Who will entertain Lex Wilde while we're closeted here?"

"Your Mr. Wilde was changing when I left the guest-house," said Chan. "We can trust him to Vong until the din-ner bell." He turned back to the vestibule, to spring the lock. "That's only in case he follows his celebrated nose for news. What I'm about to demonstrate is for your eyes alone."

John took one of the lab stools, and hooked a heel at the rung. Since their student days, it had been Chan who had lectured (by the book, or without it) while John had listened.

"Hasn't Indra shown me everything?"

"All *I've* done is set the stage," the girl said quickly.

"Has Chan made some kind of breakthrough?"

"Let's call it a long leap forward—with headaches still to come."

"If Chan's hit a bull's-eye, I'd advise him to keep his

34

notes a secret. Remember, I'm in the same business: I might steal them."

The younger Thornton had circled the table, to lay one hand on the microscope. As John had expected, he had missed the attempt at humor.

"You recognized your *Chlorella Thorntoni,* of course? That makes you a partner in my enterprise." John could not quite repress a grin, as Chan opened a bulging notebook on the table. He had expected his friend to take his collaboration for granted, even though they were, in a sense, competitors.

"Those headaches Indra mentioned just now. Am I to help solve them?"

Chan answered calmly, with his eyes on the forest of notes before him. "Why else would I use Father's illness as an excuse to get you here?"

"I guessed as much, when I saw your *bat jhow yee.*"

"*Convertor,* if you please, John. It's your own name for the apparatus. The problem we're facing is too big for jokes."

"Did your father know of this work in progress before he became ill?"

"Naturally. Algal culture has always attracted me."

"Any other confidants besides Indra?"

"Just one—Prince Ngo Singh. Naturally, I've kept him *au courant* with our work. In fact, he contributed to its upkeep, before the time of troubles in Laos."

"Does he still rule the Meo tribes?"

"With an iron hand. Even though he's been in retreat for the past year—at the Buddhist monastery. He keeps in touch through his son."

The fact that the reigning prince of the Meo knew of Chan's experiment gave it an added dimension. Considering the political eddies outside the Enchanted Valley, John was not surprised that Ngo Singh had retired to a cloister (after the example of Buddha) for rest and meditation. Recalling his own bouts of philosophy with that same nobleman, he promised himself an early call at the temple on the cliff-top.

"What was the Prince's reaction, Chan?"

"I can quote him direct. *'If what you say is true,'* he told me, *'you hold the future in your hand.'*"

John curbed a slight impatience. Knowing his friend's flair for the dramatic, he was sure Chan would unveil his surprise in his own way—or not at all.

"Those are brave words," he said mildly. "Are you about to justify them?"

"I hope so, John."

The microbiologist smiled at Indra, but the girl continued to stand with folded arms, her face a mask. Only her eyes betrayed an inner excitement as Chan turned to the nearest incubator, to remove a rack of culture tubes.

"Using your subspecies, our harvest figures are already higher than yours."

"Indra told me that much."

"Part of the increase is due to climate—and higher pressure in the convertor."

"I'll admit your apparatus is the last word."

Chan selected a tube from the rack, and took up a platinum loop to remove a drop of the medium. "I wasn't satisfied, of course. What you've seen here so far was only a beginning." As he spoke, he was skillfully preparing a hanging-drop slide.

"What were you looking for?"

"Our *sine qua non*—an increased growth-rate. I hoped to induce it with new concentrates of raw materials. Or perhaps with a higher rate of photosynthesis." Chan indicated the row of plastic blocks on the testing table. "We've spent literally months on reruns, using all the standard species: *Chlorella pyrenoidosa, Aspergillus niger, Chlorella vulgaris.* Your subspecies was still tops."

"Was?"

"The picture's changed—as you're about to observe." Chan had been focusing his hanging-drop preparation beneath a microscope. He stood back at last, motioning for John to take his place.

At first glance, the organisms in the microscopic field bore little resemblance to the species John had named for his mentor. A closer look kept his eyes glued to the oculars. If this was indeed an algal culture, its behavior was incredible, according to the known laws of growth.

36

Single cells, such as made up the lower species of algae, multiplied by division, a process whereby an individual split into two new offspring, each capable of independent life. Using the old-fashioned smear technique (which fixed dead organisms on a gram slide) biologists had frequently caught cells in this simple process of increase. During his student days John had studied countless gram slides, illustrating each stage of the life cycle; he had identified each step in this most primitive form of reproduction. Tonight he was observing living cells—and their reproduction, in all its minute detail, was taking place while he watched.

The microbiologist brushed sweat from his forehead with a shaking hand. No one, he was sure (save for Chan and his co-workers) had ever witnessed this phenomenon in a microscope. Not only was the life cycle of *Chlorella Thorntoni* completing itself before his startled gaze; the process was occurring at a fantastic tempo, like a picture-film run at many times its normal speed.

Forcing himself to concentrate on a single cell, John watched the chromatin that made up its nucleus begin to alter its skeinlike arrangement of strands and break up into dark rods that arranged themselves, with military precision, in a double row. This, he recognized, was the process whereby the ultramicroscopic units called genes (carrying the elements of heredity that gave to each cell the character of its predecessor) were also dividing. As he continued to watch the small cell, the chromosomes, as these tiny particles were called, were drawn apart by invisible strands. In a twinkling, they tumbled together again—in each half of the parent body—to form the skeinlike, patternless arrangement typical of the nucleus of a normal cell.

Even as the changes had continued in the nucleus, the cell's outer part, the cytoplasm, was also constricting at its center. As a globe might be compressed until it resembled a dumb-bell—with each of the new-formed nuclei occupying a bulbous end—so the center of the cell was narrowing rapidly. The cytoplasm was first drawn out into a taut line, then snapped. Instantly the two daughter cells thus formed assumed a perfect round, each identical with its parent.

"It's unbelievable, Chan."

John had spoken with his eyes still straining at the oculars. Now, he looked up to meet his friend's smile.

"Wasn't it worth the buildup?"

"I still can't take in what I've seen. Is this *really* an algal culture?"

"*Was* is a more exact word," said the younger Thornton. "What you've observed is a mutation, a variant from the norm. A malignancy, if you like—not too different from leukemia."

"A malignancy in *algae?*"

"You can't deny you've seen it."

John nodded a stunned agreement, then bent again to the microscope. The never ending division was crowding the hanging drop. Already he fancied the growth-rate had slowed, but he could not be sure. The regular march of the chromosomes, their retraction to form fresh nuclei, and the snapping of the cytoplasmic links, had the same nightmare precision.

"How did it happen, Chan?"

"Almost by accident. I was trying to create mutations from your original culture, using various media to jolt the cells into a faster growth-pattern. One of the agents was X ray. This was the result."

"Has it bred true?"

"We've been growing identical mutations from the first culture for over three months. I don't think it will revert. Do you?"

"No, Chan."

"You see what this could mean, of course?"

"One of the greatest discoveries in microbiology," John said slowly. "A Chlorella species that reproduces thousands of times faster than any growing thing. Prince Singh was right. You *do* hold the future in your hand."

"Naturally, part of the credit is yours."

"Does *that* matter?"

The younger Thornton ignored the question. He was striding back and forth in the center aisle, as John had often seen him do in moments of excitement. He wondered if his friend had been shaken by the violence of the thing he had created —if his comparison to leukemia had been accidental. At this very moment, the disease was draining Oscar Thornton's life away. Could it be that this exploding organism was another distortion of the life process?

"One fact is apparent," Chan said at last. "Like every change in nature, this one creates a special challenge."

"The problem of control?"

"Trust *you* to give our bugaboo a name."

John returned to his vigil at the oculars. A moment before, he had sensed that the growth-rate was slowing. Now he saw the mutation was almost at a standstill. The phenomenal cell division (proliferating at its own dizzy tempo) had used up raw materials faster than they could be supplied, with starvation as an inevitable result. The basic lack, John felt sure, was carbon dioxide, the vital agent that combined with water during photosynthesis to form the simplest of food molecules, the carbohydrates. Now that this factor was lacking, Chan's miniature food-factory was grinding to a halt.

Starvation was not the only phenomenon occurring in the hanging drop. In its center, John noted a spot of brightness, a highlight that stood out vividly in the massed cell bodies. He knew it was either air or gas—the latter, most likely, since gas was an inevitable by-product. Sensing the cause of Chan's dilemma (and a possible solution), he did not voice his thought. It was too soon to speculate on a cure.

"The big snag," he said carefully, "is the way your culture outgrows its medium."

"It's our first problem," said Chan. He was pacing the aisle again, banging his palm with soft, incessant blows. "It could be our *only* problem. If we eliminate that damned slowdown, we can harness the whole process. It could be my chance— *our* chance—to be immortal."

"It's still a big if."

"Not now, John; not when you've crossed half the world to help me."

"Methane's the death agent, isn't it?"

Indra's quick, indrawn breath, as she continued to stand in the shadows, was his answer.

"How did you know?"

"We've all waded in backwaters where algae form pond scum. When they end their life cycle and join the mud below, their death produces methane gas. It often bubbles from the bottom. I've bottled it, on biology field trips."

"Have you had this reaction in your own experiments?" Chan asked.

"Not on this scale. In San Francisco, we never worked with algae that grew under these conditions. Still, the bubble forming in this hanging drop *must* be methane gas. Since everything in your mutation develops so rapidly, methane would do the same."

"Surely we can control it," Indra said.

Again John withheld a direct answer. "Dud Porter's a genius at such problems," he said carefully. "I'll ask him to join me here in any case—on the eleventh-hour chance he'll come up with a new drug to help Papa Oscar. There's no reason why he can't bring the latest convertor equipment as well—"

Indra's voice cut into his recital: it was a high, taut note of thanksgiving:

"Do you mean it, John?"

"Of course. Meanwhile, we'll review the whole spectrum and see if we can find a lead."

"When do we start?" Chan asked.

"Why not at once?"

"You've been airborne for two days," Indra said quickly. "Won't you need rest?"

"Don't use the word, when a job like this is waiting."

Chan moved to the table's head. Even at that moment of dazed acceptance, John could not help noting how readily his friend had taken charge. And yet, when Chan held out his hands to them both, he felt a brief surge of resentment vanish without pain.

"The three of us together, just like the old days," Chan said. "What shall we call our experiment?"

"Why not Food Unlimited?" Indra asked.

"An excellent working title. We'll lay out the first schedule now."

A light but insistent knock on the outer door broke their solemn mood. Indra moved to answer the summons.

"Reality intrudes on our vision, it seems," said the younger Thornton. "Perhaps it's just as well, since we seem to have forgotten dinner completely." He snapped off the lights and led John to the inner room, closing and locking the double doors. "You'll keep this demonstration to yourself, of course?"

"That goes without saying."

"Your Mr. Wilde is bound to ask questions."

"I can handle Lex."

"What will you tell him of my work?"

"Only that you're experimenting with algae."

"So are many others. Let's hope he doesn't grow suspicious—"

"Alexander Wilde is *always* suspicious, Chan. He has to be, to hold his job."

"There's no need to mention details."

"No need whatever."

A hospital orderly waited outside the laboratory. Indra, who stood with a hand on the doorknob, moved aside to let Chan pass. A quick exchange followed in Lao, a language John no longer understood, save for a few phrases.

"It seems I'm needed in surgery," said Chan. "They've brought in an accident case from the mountain."

"I'll be glad to assist," John offered.

"Someone should check out the lab."

"I'll take care of that," said Indra. "We've been lecturing John for hours. It's time he proved he's still a doctor."

"Perhaps he'll be needed at that," said Chan, and led the way to the hospital.

Following at his heels, John heard the laboratory door shut. He could understand the click of the falling lock: the stocky figure of Lex Wilde had just risen from a chair on the clinic porch. . . . He was grateful when the journalist stood aside to give both doctors access to the surgery. Concentrating on the emergency that awaited them, he accepted the courtesy with a nod; the grilling would come later. Lex knew how to bide his time—now that tomorrow's column had been radioed to the States.

The two litter-bearers who had brought in the patient waited just inside the door: both were stocky peasants, dressed in identical black smocks and burlap-wrapped clogs. The *médecin indo-chinois* was addressing them in quick Chinese when Chan joined the discussion. Moving to the patient, who lay on an improvised stretcher, John hardly noticed the thrust and parry of the dialogue.

He saw that Dr. Vong had removed the temporary dressing. The wound was in the left thigh—a simple incision, though a deep one. Bleeding had been controlled by a makeshift tourniquet.

"What did they tell you, Chan?" John asked when his friend joined him.

"The fellow's a Kha. He was wounded in a brush with Meo herdsmen."

"The wound isn't too dangerous—unless the femoral artery's involved."

"Vong will prep him. Have you kept your hand in as a surgeon?"

"I still give a weekday to a clinic at San Francisco General."

When the doctors had finished scrubbing, John was faintly surprised at the air of tension in the surgery. Part of it, he felt sure, was caused by the presence of the two stretcher-bearers, who still stood against the far wall, with folded arms. About to order the men from the room, John shrugged off the intrusion. There was no time to pause for nonessentials.

As his friend had remarked, the patient was a Kha tribesman. (John would have recognized the man by the silver bands at his neck. It was the custom of these people to carry their entire wealth upon their bodies.) The Kha, he reminded himself, were one of many ethnic groups that made up the local population. Originally slaves, they had once been treated as beasts of burden, and even Papa Oscar's long rule in the Valley had not stamped out their persecution.

En route to the operating table, Chan paused to check the contents of the emergency tray. The native doctor had already slipped a needle into the wounded man's arm, to begin an injection of sodium pentothal.

42

"He's all yours, Dr. Merchant," said the younger Thornton. "I've never cared for the scalpel."

"What was the premedication?"

"Demorol and atropine, Doctor," said the *médecin indo-chinois*. "The Kha are opium eaters. Their tolerance for morphine is high, so I don't often use it with them."

Completing his examination of the wound, John nodded his approval. From what he could observe, the blood vessel involved was on the outer side of the thigh: since the femoral artery appeared undamaged, he could risk a complete repair-job with no danger of gangrene. The diagnosis was confirmed when Dr. Vong loosened the emergency tourniquet. The flow of blood was moderate, and could be controlled with a pressure dressing while he sutured the gash, which, he surmised had been made with either a knife or a spear. He was turning to thread a needle when the native doctor spoke sharply.

"He is failing fast, Dr. Merchant!"

There was urgent reason for the warning, John saw at once. Since the tourniquet had been loosened, the injured man's breathing had grown shallow and hurried. The pulse, which had seemed almost regular, was now both racing and thready. Most startling of all was the sudden coldness of the skin, the long, shuddering chills that racked the patient's body.

It had been years since John had coped with an emergency complication during surgery. Fortunately, the pattern of circulatory collapse, unnatural coldness and respiratory failure pointed to a familiar cause. He had seen similar cases when he had gone with Oscar Thornton on a tour of the hills and watched him deal with the aftermaths of spear wounds. He would never forget those dramatic recoveries, following an injection from the doctor's medical bag.

Later, Papa Oscar had described the effects of aconite, the poison produced from the juices of monkshood, a cowl-like flower that grew in profusion on the lower mountain slopes. Obviously the weapon that had inflicted the present wound had been dipped in the same deadly mixture. The tourniquet had saved the patient's life up to now, but its premature

43

loosening had precipitated the mixture into the bloodstream.

"Two ampules of digitoxin, quick!" John barked the order as he reknotted the tourniquet. "Leave in that needle, Dr. Vong. We'll inject directly."

Chan, understanding the problem at once, rushed to the cabinet—while John adjusted the mask of a small anesthetic machine over the patient's face, twirled the valve to inflate the breathing bag, and began to force oxygen into the lungs of the dying man. Vong had already removed his pentothal syringe; he held the intravenous needle steady in the vein until Chan could fill a second syringe with the digitoxin. In less than a minute the powerful heart stimulant (the only known antidote for aconite) was flowing directly into the bloodstream. Dr. Vong, at John's signal, continued to drive oxygen into the lungs, pressing the bag in a hard, rhythmic pattern to speed the intake.

All these moves had been made fluently, by hands that knew their tasks. It was several moments before John could be sure the life on the table had been saved. When he stood back at last, he was dimly aware that the two coolies, obeying a natural curiosity, had moved forward to check the foreign doctor's prowess. Chan spoke a command, and the men left the surgery.

John reached for the patient's pulse. As he had hoped, it had steadied under the stimulus of the injection and the charge of oxygen that had prevented complete collapse.

"I think he's out of danger now," Chan said.

"So do I—but we nearly lost him."

"How did it happen?"

John pulled off gloves and gown, and donned a fresh set. "It's got to be aconite poisoning. That sudden chill was our warning. We can discontinue artificial respiration—he's breathing almost naturally."

The surgery was routine, the ligation of a small artery in the depths of the incision. A dozen stitches were needed to close the wound. When John had tied off the last suture, Chan passed him a syringe of penicillin, which he injected liberally into the muscles below and above the injury. Before he could apply a dressing, color had returned to the patient's

44

cheeks. A moment later, he opened his eyes to look about, in silent wonder that he was still alive.

"Vong can manage the rest," Chan said.

"Aren't you going to ask the coolies how he was wounded?"

"I know already, John."

The younger Thornton joined the microbiologist at the scrub basins, a move that permitted them to face away from the surgery, where Dr. Vong still bustled about the clean-up phase of the emergency. The two coolies (lynx-eyed shadows against the night) continued to watch from the porch.

"I'm sorry this turned up so quickly," said Chan. "You've heard quite enough for a few hours in Muong Toa. I'd hoped to explain the rest at my leisure."

"This isn't the first Kha we've patched up after a fracas in the hills."

Chan's eyes narrowed, accenting the Oriental slant of the heavy brows above them. It was a look John remembered well. His friend was usually vexed when he failed to keep pace with his free-striding thoughts.

"Don't pretend you haven't noticed changes," he said. "I'm sure you've suspected others. Those traction cases in the ward, for example—"

"Have you begun a new building project?"

"The Valley runs itself these days," Chan said. "My work is centered in the lab, as you've just seen. Those cases came from the far side of the Gates—the *Chinese* side."

"Do you take Communist patients?"

"We take *patients*, John—without labels. This is the only modern clinic in a hundred miles. Most of them would die if they weren't brought in promptly."

"What caused the injuries?"

"They're blasting for a power dam. On the north face of Butterfly Mountain, in Yunnan Province. The main water-catch will be only a few miles from the border."

"How do the cases reach you?"

"I pick up most of them myself, using the trail through the Gates. There's a checkpoint at the border: our Land Rovers make fairly good ambulances. When they recover, they return by the same route."

45

"Does your father know you take such patients?"

"We've always followed that practice. When there was an active war in Laos, casualties were welcomed here—from both sides. We've yet to turn a sick man away, or a hungry one."

"You still haven't explained the spear wound, Chan."

"The engineers on that power dam pay good wages for outside help. Naturally they've recruited labor in our hill towns."

"Not among the Meo."

"True. The Meo have always hated the Chinese. This is how they hit back."

"Then there *is* friction on the border."

"There have always been frictions, John. When the dam is finished, I expect things to settle down. At the moment, as you know, there's even a truce of sorts in Laos."

"A phony cease-fire, you mean."

"Eventually we may have a *modus vivendi*."

"Laos could also be overrun tomorrow. *You* could be next."

"This valley has sat out other wars," said Chan, with the same baffling calm. "The real pressure's bound to come elsewhere. Our terrain is much too rugged for invasion."

There was no way to combat such candor, John reflected, no words to express a persistent conviction that something had been left unsaid. Obviously there was no need to remind his friend that the colossus to the north could crush all the Valley stood for, as casually as a juggernaut. The Thorntons had lived a long time in that juggernaut's shadow—and the Valley still prospered. Today, he could accept Chan's calm appraisal at face value.

"Shall we get back to the lab?"

"Aren't you ready to join Mr. Wilde at dinner? Indra ordered *coq au vin* in your honor."

"Dinner can wait, Chan, as far as I'm concerned. It doesn't seem important, now we're about to produce Food Unlimited."

# 2.

ON his first night in the Enchanted Valley, John had expected to be plagued by the dreams appropriate to a man of destiny. After a late supper at the guesthouse, he had resumed a conference in the lab that had lasted until midnight; before he had gone to his Spartan cot, he had stopped at the hospital, to give Oscar Thornton his first dose of Six-MP. Then with no more formal preparation than the removal of shoes and tie, he had slept blissfully for eight full hours.

The sun was well up when he wakened. Years of slavery to an alarm clock reproached him in the first confused moments between sleep and full consciousness, until he recalled the work schedule he had plotted with Chan. He was not due at the convertor until noon.

After the icy tonic of his shower, he donned fresh hospital whites and relaxed a moment more in his room—listening to the muted sounds from the kampong, reveling in his discovery that morning in Muong Toa was still proof that time is a dream. The chant of barter at the kitchen door told him the gate had long since been opened. From the mission school, the hilarity of young voices suggested that the process of learning was still as painless as he remembered. There was vast reassurance in these homely sounds. Already, they had made the vague fears of the night seem fantastic indeed.

The dining room of the guesthouse was empty when John entered. It was good to have the room to himself, to sit at his old window-table and refuse to think at all, until his shift began at the lab. The flower garden Chan's mother had started years ago was just outside. Hummingbirds no larger than bees were feeding in the yellow champac blossoms; the damask roses that had been Chin-ling's pride were already in bud, and a prodigal burst of English honeysuckle (flowering ahead of season) filled the room with its fragrance.

The garden set its seal on the tranquil day, making the visitor's homecoming complete. He finished a hearty breakfast with good appetite and was lighting a cigarette when Lex Wilde joined him.

"For a doctor whose only patient is dying," said the journalist, "you look uncommonly satisfied."

John refused the bait. "I'll order your food. After all that copy-chasing yesterday, I can't blame you for oversleeping."

Wilde took a facing chair, and reached for the coffee urn. The bush jacket he was wearing, along with the jungle boots and outsize whipcord breeches, completed the picture of a newshawk gone to earth.

"I didn't oversleep," he said. "If you must know, I've been visiting that settlement outside the compound."

"I hope you found what you came for. It's always picturesque on a market day."

"Scenery's cheap in these parts. So are pie-plate faces that refuse to talk your language. Or should I say, refuse to talk at all?"

"Perhaps the natives didn't understand your questions."

Wilde flushed. "I covered this backwoods when it was still French. I've press awards to prove I covered it well."

"Could you speak the hill dialects?"

"I had interpreters—on *those* field trips. The powers-that-be refused me one at Chiang Mai."

"If you'd listened to reason, you'd never have left Bangkok."

"That's no way for one friend to address another."

"Don't ruffle your feathers at me, Lex. Just take my word there isn't a scrap of news here. Not as you'd use the term."

"Last night, I sent out a full column on the shortwave. What's known as a color story. I slugged it *Utopia Limited.*"

"Was it favorable?"

"Extremely. I gave credit where credit is due. Oscar Thornton did an amazing job here. Apparently his reforms have stood the test of time. The burning question remains: How long can Utopia last?"

"Indefinitely, I hope."

"With a half-billion empty bellies rumbling next door?"

48

"Chan thinks geography will protect the Valley—just as it's always done."

"I'll admit your friend's an old China hand," said Wilde. "I still can't accept such easy answers. My job is to develop fresh viewpoints."

"Including the specter of enemy invasion?"

"How do you explain that wounded Kha?"

"Who told you he'd been wounded?"

"I may not speak the hill dialects, John: I do know a little Cantonese. Those litter-bearers were Chinese. The fellow they carried was struck down by a spear. It was thrown by some-one who resented the money he's been earning across the border. Doesn't that show Oscar Thornton's Shangri-La is about to explode?"

"All it shows is that the Meo and the Kha enjoy fighting."

"In Bangkok, I heard the local prince is the only bar to all-out warfare. How can he hold the line from a monastery?"

John kept his patience and his temper. "The temporal ruler of the Meo is their spiritual lord as well. Prince Ngo Singh could make his orders stick, even if he were in exile. If he says the Valley's neutral, neutrality's the fashion."

The journalist shrugged. "Yesterday the Thornton house-boy drove me halfway to Butterfly Mountain. I wanted to visit the monastery, but he said it was off limits."

"On Ngo Singh's orders, I'm sure."

"Before we turned back, I had a fair view of that notch you called the Gates of Hell. Would it interest you to learn we were near enough to hear rockblasting?"

"Chan tells me they're building a power dam in Yunnan."

"Will you join me in a private look across the border, if I can bribe a guide?"

"I'm a scientist, Lex, not a cloak-and-dagger man."

"Don't pretend you came here only to see Oscar Thorn-ton into the next world. You're also hatching something with his son."

John rose from the table with a yawn and strolled to the window. He had anticipated this attack. With Chan's ap-proval, he had prepared to meet it.

"Just what are you after now?" he asked.

"Last night you skipped a damned good dinner to go back to that laboratory. You stayed until midnight, behind locked doors. Will you tell me why?"

"The natives are convinced Chan keeps his private devils in that building. Naturally he keeps the doors padlocked."

"Don't expect me to buy that mumbo jumbo."

"You'll find the devils well bottled," John said easily. "Choose your own time. Chan or Indra will give you a guided tour."

"And leave me no wiser than before?"

"Probably—unless you've a degree in biology."

"Since you're being so openhanded, why not give me a run-down of Thornton's work in progress?"

"This month, he's studying a transplantable tumor in mice —showing the specificity of the virus that causes it. He's still working hard on serum coagulation tests to diagnose preclinical leukemia. He's also running a series on the photosynthetic behavior of various forms of algae."

Lex had been taking notes automatically. Now, holding his copy paper at arm's length, he frowned at his faultless shorthand.

"Those last two are your special subjects. Is this a coincidence?"

"Chan and I were students together. Our interests have always coincided."

"Last night he told me he had a complete file of your publications. Did that surprise you?"

"Not at all. Cross-filing the literature is standard practice in our trade. Other researchers have done the same."

"What has *he* published lately?"

John had expected this question too. "You'd know of his work on jungle typhus, if you'd read the French journals. Last year, he did a definitive study of opium addiction among the Kha."

"Did either of those papers break new ground?"

"All of us can't be earthshakers, Lex. The spadework done by the Chan Thorntons is vital to biology. There could be no real discoveries without it."

50

The journalist rose to his feet with an elaborate yawn that did not quite disguise his frustration.

"I know you think your half-caste friend is perfect," he said. "Don't tell me he isn't human too. In his place, I'd envy you like sin. I'd probably hate you in the bargain."

"What right have you to make that inference?"

"Put yourself in his place, John. He's about to take over in this valley—from one of our few remaining saints. Can he top what his father's done here? As a researcher, he's been just another graduate whizbang with a bump of curiosity, and no real flair. Will his name go down in history, as yours is sure to?"

"Spare the praise, please, until I've earned it."

"Facts are facts," said Wilde. "When you leave Muong Toa, you'll return to a career that adds up, on all fronts. What can *he* look forward to—except a ride down a Chinese drainpipe?"

With an effort, John kept his indulgent smile in place. The journalist had summarized his thoughts all too shrewdly: a fast retreat was essential.

"None of those questions deserve answers, Lex."

"Here's one you can't avoid. How long will you stay here?"

"That depends on my patient."

"I looked in at the hospital this morning. They told me there was no change."

"The drug I'm using sometimes slows the progression of leukemia markedly. It can't cure the disease."

"In other words, you're standing a deathwatch."

"You might call it that, I suppose."

"And you're giving young Thornton a hand with his research while you wait?"

"I'll do what I can, of course."

"Including a radiogram to Dud Porter—ordering additional equipment?"

John forced a chuckle to mask his anger. "With a first-rate lab at my disposal here, I can't afford to neglect my own work entirely. Besides, Dud will be bringing drugs that may help Oscar Thornton."

"He could even be bringing the answer to your dream."

51

"I'm a biologist, Lex. I don't have time for dreams."

"Isn't it true that your crowd has been trying to turn algae into a cheap food-factory? Suppose you brought off that miracle in Muong Toa—who'd get the credit?"

"You've a long day ahead. Don't let your imagination go berserk."

The journalist sighed and moved toward the door, where he paused to level an accusing finger. "Keep up the smoke screen, if you like. I'll get behind it soon enough."

"If I insist I'm hiding nothing, will you believe me?"

"Frankly, no. Will you promise me an exclusive when the big break comes, if I'll leave you in peace pro tem?"

"Is that a bargain?"

Wilde extended his hand, and shook John's firmly. His palm was bathed in sweat: despite himself, John found he was admiring the man's tenacity.

"You'll be the first to hear, Lex, if we make real news in Chan's lab. Will that hold you?"

"It will have to, for the present. Do me one more favor, and I'll promise to stay clear of the windows."

"If I can."

"Set up an interview with Prince Ngo Singh."

"I've been told he's in complete seclusion."

"He'll see *you,* won't he?"

"That's hardly the same as meeting the press. After all, we're old friends."

"Do you plan to visit him soon?"

"Of course. Protocol demands it."

"I dare you to make that visit." Lex Wilde paused for the last word. "We both know he can answer every question you've refused to face. About Chan Thornton—and his kingdom. Will you have the courage to ask them?"

When John crossed the compound to the laboratory, he found Indra waiting at the door.

"I looked into the dining room just now," she said. "Did you enjoy your breakfast?"

"I've known Lex a long time. He couldn't spoil my appetite."

52

"Has he guessed what we're working on?"

"As of now, he hasn't a notion."

The girl took a folded paper from the pocket of her uniform. "This just came for you—on the airfield radio. I couldn't help reading it."

John scanned the radiogram. It was a reply to his message to San Francisco. The Station laboratory advised him that most of the equipment he requested was already assembled. Dr. Dudley Porter would be leaving before the day ended. Weather permitting, he would touch down at Hong Kong in two days' time, fly to Chiang Mai with his airfreight, and await a pickup.

"Your man Friday is efficient," said Indra.

"Magic carpets are things Dud takes for granted. I hope his journey's worthwhile."

"I helped Chan with the first run this morning. He feels we're on the edge of a breakthrough. Don't you back his judgment?"

John hesitated. Stirred by the warmth of her voice, he longed to describe the solution that had come to him while he studied the life-and-death cycles of the Chlorella mutation. Again he warned himself to hold his tongue, until he could test that flash of intuition against Dud Porter's hard common sense.

"Last night I promised to do all I could," he said carefully. "I refuse to hold out false hopes."

"You realize what this will mean, if we push it through?"

"To Chan? Or to humanity in general?"

"Right now, I'm thinking first of him."

A question hung on John's lips: he released it, without taking thought.

"Why haven't you two married, Indra? I've expected a wedding announcement for years."

"Don't the women in America wait until they're asked? They do in Muong Toa."

"Do you have an understanding?"

"Yes and no. Chan feels he's unready for marriage—until he's accomplished something real here, in his own right."

"Did he say that?"

"Not in so many words, but it's part of his credo. It's kept him wedded to a microscope. In his heart, he knows he'll succeed or fail there."

"And you've accepted the situation?"

"I was content to leave things as they were—to help all I could." Indra had colored under John's look, but her voice was steady. "The year you left us, I was ready to marry him, for Papa Oscar's sake. I'm still prepared, if he finds he needs me. I'll even pretend I love him."

"Did you say *pretend?*"

"Surely you've guessed why I've . . . refused to meet you halfway. I suppose it's old-fashioned of me, but I'm the kind of woman who gives her heart but once."

Shaken though he was by the declaration, John kept his head. The temptation to take Indra in his arms, in full view of the compound, had almost engulfed him: summoning his willpower, he forced himself to speak calmly.

"The debt to Papa Oscar remains, then?"

"Now more than ever—for us both. Surely you can see that."

"Would he want you to marry Chan if you didn't love him?"

"What's important now is Muong Toa, and what it has meant to the world. They didn't just give a Nobel Prize to Oscar Thornton. They gave it to the ideal he created here, and what that ideal means. If I can help keep it alive, and Chan still wants me, I'm where I belong."

"Years ago Papa Oscar told me Chan needed you as a balance wheel. What if that need no longer existed? What if he brings in an algal culture that will link his name with Pasteur —and make him a whole man at last? Would your answer to me be different?"

Indra had regained her poise: the flashing smile she offered John as she re-entered the laboratory would have graced any *femme du monde*.

"In that case, Dr. Merchant, you might remember Longfellow's poem. The one that dealt with Miles Standish and John Alden."

A little later, when he followed Indra to the vestibule,

John's heartbeat had steadied. He still pretended to fumble with the padlock before closing the door behind him.

Even by daylight, he saw, the long workrooms were shuttered, their automatic air conditioners purring gently, their neons bathing the tables in flawless light. In the far room, a native technician was repeating the injection of a dozen white mice. Another was hard at work above the plastic blocks. The microbiologist paused beside the microtome to chat for an instant with the diminutive Annamese who was mounting a series of slides, with a skill that suggested long training.

In the alcove beyond the half-open panels, he could hear the steady pulsation of the *bat jhow yee*. Chan would be at his post, timing the monster's heartbeat: Indra would be seated at the table's head, taking notes at his dictation. Last midnight, when they had made preparations for today's run, the solar convertor had seemed as potent as the sea beast it resembled. This noon, bathed in the pitiless light of reality, John found it as commonplace as an outsize laundromat, and quite as limited in its function. By what process of self-delusion had he convinced himself that this steel-and-plastic complex could change the history of the world?

The sudden depression, he knew, was an automatic reflex. The convertor, after all, was only a token apparatus, a harbinger of things to come: with Dud Porter's mechanical genius to back him, there was every hope that Chan's rampaging mutation could be mastered—fulfilling Prince Ngo Singh's solemn prediction that they held the future in their hands. Chan Thornton would find his belated fulfillment, when the experiment had proved its worth. Once they had achieved success in that alcove, the bonds that held Indra to Muong Toa would be broken forever.

It was a strange deliverance for the woman he desired, but John could remind himself (not too grimly) that all was fair in love and war. If Chan meant to use his talents without mercy, he would return the compliment. The panting of the convertor still suggested a laundromat when he joined the others in the alcove, but he was humming a contented tune when he took his place at the worktable.

The days that followed that first morning in the lab soon fell into an unchanging pattern. Once his course was set, John found he could follow it dutifully—and almost without thought.

He slept late each morning (a habit that permitted him to avoid Lex Wilde). After breakfast, he paid one of his three daily visits to Oscar Thornton's bedside. Later he reworked his notes, or walked for an hour on one of the mountain trails. Sharp at noon, he relieved Chan or Indra in the alcove, to continue their tabulations until dusk. By the third day, he confessed that his observations had merely confirmed things he already knew.

Until his discovery of the X-ray mutation, Chan's careful plodding had not really progressed beyond John's own research on the far side of the globe. The microbiologist had already admitted the greater capacity of his friend's convertor and the ingenuity of its plastic exposure, but these were only questions of degree. The increased yield of dried algae (an impressive advance over his best harvest in San Francisco) was still far from decisive: the mutation itself, as he had feared, proved a stubborn antagonist on each test run.

Before the first day ended, he saw that the new species had inexorably established a physical limit, beyond which it could not be pushed. In the States, he had followed something of the same baffled gambit with his own *Thorntoni:* the present algal culture had merely canceled out its speeded growth-rate with its capacity for self-destruction. Blank walls of this sort, the microbiologist admitted, had discouraged most researchers in the field: they explained why these green chemical factories (so promising in the beginning) had been largely abandoned. Only his bargain with Indra—and his stubborn belief that a solution was almost in his grasp—kept him at Chan's worktable.

Control was the key, John told himself, not only to the runaway growth-pattern, but to the mutation's premature death in its own miasma. Chan's convertor, in its present form, could never solve those matching problems. Until the third day of his tabulations, it had not occurred to him that the *bat jhow yee* itself could be a deadly menace.

He had followed Chan's routines meticulously during his shifts in the alcove, using the batches of culture medium his friend had prepared in the vat, and tabulating the yields with patient skill. On the afternoon of that third day, the lab was deserted, save for a native technician, who was preparing tissue slides at a microtome in the main room. Chan had gone to the hills on another errand, and Indra was teaching at the nurses' school. Mixing his first batch of mutation, setting the intake hose for a new test run, John had been delighted at his chance to dominate the scene on his own.

For this run he had used a far stronger blend of mutation and nutrient, hoping to please Chan with an increased harvest. The change in the convertor was apparent, even before the plastic tubes had distended fully.

It was the warmest hour of the day, and the sun was blazing in a cobalt sky: under the prod of the rheostat, the pump was operating at full speed. The rhythm, though an exciting one, seemed no different from a hundred similar tests John had clocked in his own laboratory. Bit by bit, he increased the flow of raw materials from the vat until every fiber of the great, many-legged octopus was throbbing with solar energy. It was the first time he had seen the convertor extended to its capacity: while the tempo lasted, he could almost believe the monster was his ally.

His triumph was brief. Almost without warning the pump was laboring like an overtaxed heart, and John's trained ear had pinned down the cause. In that brief period, the growth of the cells had outpaced the capacity of the plastic coils. As a result, the culture medium had begun to back up in the convertor, clogging the pump itself.

The problem had an apparent solution. By diluting the mixture in the tubes, the operator could slow the runaway growth-rate. John opened the water valve without even pausing for thought, holding it at its highest pressure until the pump had resumed its even throbbing.

Again the relief was short-lived: he saw at once that he had solved one problem only to create another. The amount of nutrient available to the fast-dividing algae had been lessened by dilution. Now, as the life cycle slowed, the forces

57

of degeneration raced to their climax, just as they had done under the microscope.

It was uncanny to observe the same phenomenon in these plastic coils, to realize this was an identical pattern of decay, magnified beyond computation. The pump still labored mightily, in a futile effort to circulate the now-inert mixture. Shrugging in exasperation at his error, John disengaged the electric switch, bringing the whole mechanism to a grinding halt. Yet, though the convertor itself was silent, its massive, dead-white tentacles continued to rise and swell as ominously as before.

Dumbfounded at the mutation's power to destroy itself, John recalled the spot of light he had observed in the center of the hanging drop. In that flash of perception, he realized that each cell in these distended tubes, moving toward death at a dizzy tempo, was producing its own minute quantity of highly explosive methane gas. Unless that pressure was relieved, Chan's laboratory might be blown sky-high.

There was an access door to the outside, set in the retaining wall of the skylight. John flung it wide to check the condition of the tubes in the court, only to learn that they, too, were distended alarmingly. Returning to the main lab, he shouted a warning to the technician which sent the man scurrying to safety, unscrewed the razor-sharp blade of the microtome, and ran back to the court. By now the tentacles of the *bat jhow yee* were swollen to a monstrous caricature, but even as he waited for the first detonation, John kept his head.

With quick strokes of the blade, he slashed at each plastic segment. By design, the walls of the tubes were paper-thin, to admit the sunlight on which the octopus fed. The knife, he saw, had performed its surgery with time to spare.

John leaned against the skylight, gasping for breath in the choking clouds of methane, shielding his face against the sprays of musty Chlorella culture. Then, as the hissing subsided, he knew the deadly gas had diluted itself in the open air, before it could back up to the furnace and be ignited.

Enough of the methane had reached his lungs to threaten him with asphyxiation. He was only half-aware of his actions

58

when he reeled back to the alcove and bent above the grille of a conditioner to gulp fresh air. Then, still staggering from the aftermath of his escape, he felt Indra's arm around his shoulder, and leaned against her while she led him to a chair.

"It's a miracle I'm still alive," he said dazedly. "I'm not sure I deserve it."

"Don't talk for a moment, John."

He breathed deep, with his head still on her shoulder. The contact was grateful: he had no wish to break it.

"I'll tell you I'm sorry, when my head stops spinning," he offered.

"Didn't you realize there was enough methane in those tubes to destroy the whole building?"

"I realize it now."

"How did the backup start?"

"I decided to step up the mixture."

"With *mutated* algae?"

John managed a sheepish grin—and rose from the chair. Objects on the facing shelves had ceased to whirl in circles.

"Fortunately I realized what I'd done. I hope the convertor isn't too badly damaged."

"We've slit the tubes before to relieve pressure. It was a brave thing you did, John. You might have suffocated in that alcove."

"I hadn't much choice, with a whole lab at stake."

"After this, are you sure you want to go on?"

"Now more than ever. It's too soon to go into details, but what just happened could help Dud Porter answer our problem."

"A message came in at the airstrip this noon. Your assistant's been delayed in Hong Kong."

"That's good news too. He can pick up some extra equipment I'll be needing." Turning to Indra while he fought down a last wave of dizziness, John found they were in each other's arms, there in the doubtful shelter of the alcove. The quick meeting of their lips, and the girl's sudden gasp as she broke free, seemed part of his waking mirage.

"Perhaps this thing has gone far enough," said Indra.

"I hope I don't understand you."

"This near-explosion may be a warning, John. Papa Oscar can't live more than a few days. You can still give up and go home."

"I don't frighten that easily," he said. "Nor do you. Have you forgotten what's at stake if we do succeed?"

When the younger Thornton returned at dusk, John was ready with his findings. His friend accepted the accident with good humor, and promised the technicians would repair the damaged tubes by morning. Already, John could see that he expected Dud Porter to bring a miracle in his baggage. Chan's only real concern, he gathered, was the prodding of Lex Wilde.

"Someday I'll reward you for muzzling that bulldog," he said. "After his first twenty-four hours in the compound, I was prepared to ship him out. Thanks to you, he's been fairly reasonable since."

"Lex will sit tight," John said. "He believed me when I promised him a scoop, if and when one develops."

"Have you any doubt it will?"

"In our business, Chan, we're supposed to doubt until the last trump."

"Speaking of Wilde, how can he linger here day after day without copy? Doesn't he have three weekly columns to fill, all over America?"

"So far, he hasn't missed a deadline. He can still discuss the future of man—even while he's camped on your doorstep. World brotherhood and the United Nations are his two prime subjects. Listen long enough, and you'd think he invented both."

"Yesterday he told me his editor insisted he stay on—so he could write Father's eulogy on the spot. It's what the working press calls a deathwatch."

"Lex doesn't pull his punches, Chan. He expects to file *that* story any day now."

The appraisal was realistic, and John made it with a heavy heart. Papa Oscar's medication had promised well at first. For the first two days, the gradual process of failing had been arrested, though the patient had shown no real improvement.

Later, the progressive breakup of body tissue had begun anew. Now it was grimly evident that Six-MP could not reverse the trend. John had no real hope that the experimental drugs Dudley Porter was bringing could do more.

A short but violent rainsquall (spinning north from the flanks of the spring monsoon) invaded the Enchanted Valley on the fourth day of John's visit, making the higher trails impassable. On the fifth morning, he had risen early to learn the road to the monastery was open. Protocol suggested he pay his respects to Prince Ngo Singh with no further delay.

When he left the hospital after his call on Papa Oscar (and his usual consultation with Chan), one of the Rovers was waiting at the kampong gate. It was a sturdy vehicle, combining the best features of an American jeep with the African ox-wagon. The houseboy on the front seat stepped down at his approach, and he climbed in to take the wheel. While he was warming the motor, he heard his friend's voice from the hospital porch, a shout that froze his hands to the instrument board. He guessed the reason for the summons long before he could swing the Rover across the compound.

"Is it your father, Chan?"

"Vong thinks he's emerging from coma."

The two doctors hastened down the hall to the private wing. A few moments ago, John had left his patient in this same shadowed room, in a state of near-collapse after his last transfusion. An ampule of mercaptopurine stood on the table, ready for the next dose: a native nurse was in attendance, her eyes wide with unspoken dread.

John bent above the bed for a fresh appraisal. A layman would have noted little change in Oscar Thornton's condition: the same waxen pallor prevailed, and the breathing was barely audible. John's eye, trained in all phases of this wasting disease, saw his patient was, in fact, hovering on the brink of consciousness. The faint quiver of his eyelids, the slight resistance when John moved his arm, the heightened activity of the triceps reflex, completed the clinical picture. None of this was evidence of a real upturn: John had expected no such dramatic change. It meant only that Papa Oscar's brain, like

61

a silent clock that begins to tick again for no apparent cause, was striving to make contact with externals.

"What does it mean?"

"He wants to reach us, Chan. Don't ask me how he found the strength to come back."

"The change began just after you left, according to Vong. He claims Father knew you were in the room."

The *médecin indo-chinois,* hurrying in with a syringe of coramine, spoke up indignantly.

"I am positive he spoke Dr. Merchant's name."

Oscar Thornton's voice rose from the hospital bed. Faint though the whisper was, it reached John's ears clearly.

"Dr. Vong's hearing is excellent, Chan."

The microbiologist was already at his patient's side, with a hand on his shoulder. Papa Oscar, he saw, was now fully conscious. The eyes in that parchment-white face were alive with recognition, and the lips had managed to twist into a smile.

"Don't try to talk, sir. Not if it tires you."

"I *want* to talk, John. To you especially."

Dr. Vong came forward with the syringe of coramine, but John waved the powerful stimulant aside. Medical aid, at such moments, was contraindicated: the patient's strength came from within.

"I hope you're glad to see me, Doctor?"

Oscar Thornton studied him for a moment without speaking, then put out his hand. The strength in the frail fingers was surprising.

"Why did you come back? There's no hope at all of saving me."

"*I* sent for him, Father," said Chan. "Indra and I refused to accept your diagnosis."

The patient's eyes had not moved. He seemed barely aware of the interruption.

"Perhaps it's a happy augury that you're visiting us again, John. Even if you came on a fruitless errand."

"Don't wear yourself out, sir. We can talk again when you're stronger."

The smile on the pallid lips broadened. "Let me say what's on my mind. It won't take long." The voice faded, and Papa

Oscar's eyelids fluttered briefly. "Last time you were here, if memory serves, you approved what you saw. Do you still?"

"We've been over all this, Father," said Chan.

"I know. But some things bear repeating."

"I promised to keep peace with our neighbors. Just as you have done."

"*Peace!* Tell me, John, does the word still have meaning?"

Once again, it was as though Oscar Thornton and the microbiologist were alone in the hospital room. This time there was a pleading light in the dying man's eyes that John had never seen before. It shook him, far more than he dared show.

"Nothing has changed," he said quickly. "It's the same Valley, the same happy people. We'll keep things as they are."

"*You* won't be staying here. Chan has no right to keep you."

"I expect to be in Muong Toa for some time. Chan and I are working together in his lab."

"Is this true, my son?"

"It's my algae project," Chan said soothingly. "We're pooling our knowledge to finish it."

"Since that's John's specialty, it's quite another matter. How long can he stay?"

"As long as need be," said Chan. "Am I right, John?"

"Of course."

"I'm glad to hear you say that, John," Oscar Thornton murmured. "I couldn't leave the world with better news."

"We'll have no more talk of dying, sir. You'll be with us a long time."

The man in the hospital bed chuckled: the sound was a note of his old self. "You were never a convincing liar, Dr. Merchant." The pallid lips had barely framed the words: the grip on John's hand relaxed, as his patient sank into a deep slumber.

The two doctors lingered for an instant at the bedside, before John surrendered his place to Dr. Vong. They did not speak until they stood together on the clinic porch.

"Somehow, I never expected this to happen," Chan said at last.

"Rules don't hold in these cases. He wanted to get through to us one more time. Somehow, he made it."

"It was you he wanted, not me." Chan had spoken quietly, but there was an undertone of hurt in his voice. "Is there a chance it will happen again?"

"I think not. Did I tell him what he wished to hear?"

"You always have," said the younger Thornton. "Today you surpassed yourself." He turned to the Land Rover, still parked in the shade of the hospital wing. "Weren't you planning a visit to the monastery?"

"The visit can wait."

"The Prince is expecting you to call. I'll stay with Father until noon. Vong can relieve me then."

"I won't be gone long, Chan."

"You must be back at six to take Indra's place at the convertor. We can't lose time on the test runs."

"You're right, of course."

"Now Father knows we're working together, we've a new reason to push this job through. I'm aware I've tossed most of the work in your lap so far. Starting tomorrow, I'll try to improve my score."


The unexpected return to the sickroom had left its own chill aftermath: John fought to put it from his mind as he drove through the kampong gates. After a five-year lapse, it was his first close look at the village that lay just beyond the palings of the hospital grounds.

The cluster of buildings had grown here naturally, to serve the various farms that Oscar Thornton had founded in the Valley. Bit by bit, the settlement had climbed the slopes of nearby hills: John estimated that it now housed a thousand souls. Viewed at firsthand, its sights and sounds brought back a throng of memories. Parking the Rover among the tin-roofed market stalls, closing his eyes to inhale its mingled aromas, he could believe he was a boy again.

*Toa Far Yuen*—the Valley of the Peach Blossoms. Repeating the old Manchu name, tasing its poetry on his tongue, John wondered if the picture was still valid.

Viewed objectively, the scene before him could have been lifted bodily from another century. Yellow-skinned women (in dun-colored trousers and blouses) were shopping among the stalls for smoked eels, and the fiery fish-sauce that made their glutinous "sticky rice"—the staple of so many Eastern diets—endurable. Here were sturdy Meo, tall Kha tribesmen and the so-called Black Thai from the lower valley. Here were slender Lao in their long white tunics, and Yao herdsmen from the mountains, their heads gay in tightly-wound red turbans. Some of the villagers (John felt sure) would remember Oscar Thornton's ward, but he had yet to receive a greeting. It was too much to say the car was an island, shunned by the flow of marketers, but the visitor could not escape the conviction that, even as Lex Wilde, he was a stranger here. After a five-year absence, was he just as unwelcome?

He shook off the question, kicked the starter of the car, and followed the village street to the bamboo thicket that marked the beginning of the steep trail to the monastery. The first slopes were thick with teak: in that leafy tunnel, John recovered his composure as rapidly as his hands had mastered the English shift of the Rover. In his youth, he had known every kink in this tortuous approach to the cliff-top. It pleased him to find the same prayer flags at each bend, to sniff the odor of charred earth on the higher slopes—a reminder of the Meo's fondness for "burning the mountain" to ready their fields for the spring poppy crop.

It was true that the few natives he encountered left the trail in haste, but he could blame their withdrawal on fear of the gas-combustion engine. When he reached the temple gate, faced the Rover downhill and cramped the wheels to anchor it to the road, he was glad he had sought the Prince without advance notice.

The temple's massive walls were still drowned to the eaves in moss: the stone arabesques at each corner of the roof were as intricate as he remembered them. Each of the gabled wings were carved with fantastic spirals, suggesting the tails of serpents held in mystic subjection, even as the hood of the king cobra had spread above Buddha to shelter him from the sun.

John entered through the outer gate, left ajar at this hour to receive offerings from the faithful. A pyramid of baskets stood in the shade of the gateway. The visitor dropped his own donation in the alms box, then seated himself on a bench in the shadow of a huge *dracéna*, the dragon tree that resembles the American magnolia. At his feet, a fountain made its own quiet music in a nest of lily pads. It was the traditional waiting place for the visitor, the ideal haven for a doubting spirit.

Certain that the sound of his motor had been warning enough, he made no effort to announce his arrival. In the main building, tall doors were closed on a low-pitched murmur that died while he listened. It was the closing noontime prayer, to be followed by an hour of silence and contemplation. Lost in his own thoughts, John was hardly conscious of the whisper of sandals on the worn flagstones: he looked up tardily to face the ancient, wispy-bearded monk who had emerged from the great hall. It was a man he recalled from other visits.

"Can I help you, my son?"

"If you will, my father. I wish to see the noble prince, Ngo Singh." (The ceremonial words had come naturally to John's tongue.)

"There are no princes here. Only those who find peace through the disciplines of Gautama Buddha."

"The man I seek is known outside these walls as the Chao Kueng." It was the Lao term which signified chief, or governor.

"The Chao Kueng is in contemplation. I will warn him of your presence."

John knew usage would demand that Ngo Singh wait a little longer behind those half-closed doors: he kept his place and continued to fix his eyes on the fountain, when the man he sought emerged at last. The Prince was of commanding height, with a face and head fit to be stamped on a medal. He seemed vigorous as ever and completely at ease in his saffron robes. A rapid calculation told the visitor he was now

66

almost sixty: headlines in America had reminded him of the privations Ngo Singh had suffered during the undeclared war in Laos, yet the Prince seemed tranquil as the sunlit afternoon.

"You are a welcome sight, Doctor," he murmured. "It has been years since one of your eminence has visited us here."

"I meant to come sooner, Your Highness."

"I know how busy you've been in the Valley: it's the lot of all men who join forces with Chan Thornton. Your visit is no less welcome because it is delayed." The gleam in the Prince's eye had softened the formality of his words. "You have changed much since I saw you last."

"You, too, have changed." John made the statement boldly: complete frankness had always characterized his talks with Ngo Singh. Five years ago, he had called on the Prince at his hunting lodge in the next valley, using a plane his host had provided. At the time, the Chao Kueng had been ruler of the whole district.

"Change is a word of many meanings, Doctor. Today you are a true man of the world, yet I can recognize the boy I knew from happier times. I, too, am the ruler you remember, though I devote myself to higher things than tiger hunts, and wear the robes of the One Above All."

"Will you end your days here, as a lay brother?"

The Prince seemed untroubled by John's directness. "My retreat is temporary, Doctor. Perhaps you find that hard to believe. Like your countrymen, you expect a man in my position to play an active role. To you, my withdrawal from the mainstream must seem a waste of time—which, after all, is a golden coin we spend but once."

"If my question was impertinent, I withdraw it."

The Prince's eyes were on the fountain: he did not seem to heed the apology.

"In each of the great religions," he said, "there are certain vital symbols. We Buddhists sometimes speak of the River and the Bo Tree. Life's flood-tide and the haven on the bank. These ancient walls are my Bo Tree, Dr. Merchant. Here I repair a tired spirit—until I am ready to enter the flood again."

"Do you find retirement that useful?"

"I would have been lost without this pause for reflection. Had I wished, I could have chosen another retreat. I could have lived in a French villa, and played baccarat at the casino with other self-pitying *émigrés*. Instead, I chose the one corner of my former kingdom that remains peaceful—to await a portent there. My people see I have not abandoned them."

"I was sure of that, Your Highness."

"You, of course, would await your portent in the world. That, too, is the will of God."

"Was it God's will that I return to the Valley?"

"So you seek your answer too, beneath the Bo Tree?"

"I'll admit I'm badly in need of guidance," said John. "When I arrived, I had some slight hope of saving Papa Oscar. The best I can do is prolong his life."

"And the other matter for which you were brought here?"

The shift threw John off-balance. Aware of the Prince's knowledge, he had not expected the question so soon.

"Chan tells me he has informed you of his work with algae."

"I was happy to hear he had named his discovery after his illustrious father."

"*I* named the culture, not Chan. It's true he produced a mutation from the subspecies I isolated."

"As a young man," said the Prince, "I meant to take all knowledge as my province. Today, of course, the ambition is beyond a single brain. I do have some slight knowledge of scientific method. Enough, I hope, to grasp your objective. Will you repeat its essentials, to test me?"

The Prince listened in attentive silence while John outlined the structure of the solar convertor, the biological factors underlying the growth of algae as an easily available source of food, and the hope (so far unrealized) of mastering the runaway pace of the mutation.

"Assuming this amazing cell division could be controlled," said Ngo Singh, "would the production you visualize be feasible?"

"Entirely, once we have established a workable system of operation."

68

"What would be the most logical approach?"

"Ideally, massive algae-harvests would be consumed—much as rice is now used in the Orient. There would be one tremendous difference. Rice alone produces vitamin-lack diseases like beriberi. This food contains every element of a healthy diet."

"Let me make sure I follow you, Dr. Merchant. If science mastered this process, could it banish hunger?"

"My answer was on record, long before I saw Chan's mutation. Science could feed the world—using an area for algal culture no larger than Rhode Island."

"Assuming the experiment you're conducting now is an unqualified triumph."

"I'll admit it's a massive hope."

"Surely Chan Thornton looks forward to success—after the investment he's made."

"As of now, he hopes to use the Valley as a pilot project."

"Do you feel my people would cooperate?"

"If Papa Oscar were active, I'd have no doubt of it."

"But you're not sure his son could command the same loyalty?"

"He could, if *you* backed him."

"Perhaps my help would come too late, Doctor. Cynics in your country tend to write off this corner of Asia. They feel it's doomed and damned by history."

"When you say history, do you mean China?"

"My people call the Chinese the devils of the North. Considering the inroads their rulers have made, I think the name is earned."

"Our government is doing what it can to reverse those inroads."

"Using any means short of war—because Washington fears the reaction of Moscow."

"There's some reason to believe Russia would prefer a status quo in this area, if only to improve its own position."

"Are you sure that isn't another illusion?"

"Perhaps it is, sir. I didn't come here to discuss my country's foreign policy. I *am* concerned over the consequences of my own actions. Is it foolhardy to conduct these experiments so close to an enemy border?"

The Prince studied John thoughtfully. "I remember you as a boy in Muong Toa," he said. "In those days, my people called you the Young Warrior."

"Because I used to hunt deer with a crossbow?"

"Now you return to us with the arms of science, ready to wage a different war. Do you really think I could help win it?"

"You might, if you can keep peace in this valley."

"That has been my hope from the start, Doctor. It prompted my withdrawal to this cliff-top. My people know I wish them to remain neutral, in thought and in deed, until I determine our future course."

"Suppose the Valley were invaded directly—through the Gates of Hell?"

"This land has known many invaders, Doctor. Centuries ago, the Khmer kings avenged the depredations of the Great Khan and pushed as far north as Yunnan. There have been wars with the Burmese to the west, with the Champa to the east. Each war ended in its season, and our hill tribes endured."

"Can you be sure that pattern will hold true today?"

"I won't risk an answer at present. After a generation of Thornton bounty, Muong Toa may be facing its greatest crisis. It could still prove the truth of Buddha's teaching, that in time all change becomes changeless. As things stand, I feel we've a chance to avoid strife. I'll do all I can to prevent it."

"I'd give a great deal for your detachment, sir."

Ngo Singh walked with the visitor to the outer gate where he paused, his eyes on the sunlit valley.

"If you doubted me, would you remain here another day?"

"I'm taking a calculated risk, for Chan's sake. Only today, I promised to stay on awhile. I trust his judgment of the situation—and yours—will prove sounder than mine."

"Is this the only reason you will linger?"

"I do have a second motive, Your Highness."

"The girl called Indra Lal?"

"If things turn out as I hope, she'll return with me to America, as my wife."

"Was this *le père* Oscar's wish?"

"At the beginning, he had other plans for her. As you just remarked, time changes all things, if one is patient."

"So it does, Dr. Merchant. At least, his wishes belong with yesterday. It seems he died while we sat talking here."

"What are you saying?"

"Look into the valley, if you doubt me."

John stepped quickly through the monastery gate. A glance down the mountain road was enough to show the Prince's remark had not been clairvoyance. An hour ago, on the hospital roof, a flag had whipped bravely at its standard. Now it hung at half-mast in the windless air of noon.

# 3.

TAKING the swivel chair behind the desk, Chan motioned John to a seat on the ancient horsehair couch in the consulting room. The gesture put a neat period on Oscar Thornton's final illness. For more than six months, John reminded himself, Chan had ruled the Enchanted Valley as his father's deputy. Inevitably he had taken on a new dimension, now the authority was his alone.

"Were you shocked by the pyre, John?"

"Only at first."

"My mother's body was consumed in the same fashion. Her ashes were scattered on the fields. Tomorrow the whole valley will perform that ceremony a second time."

"Making them *both* one with Asia?"

"It was my father's wish, from the day he set foot here. He even mentioned it in his will."

John closed his eyes on a last prayer for the dead. Behind the lids, he could vision the tower of flame that had just subsided on the hillside. His ears could still hear the crackle of burning deodar logs, the low, wailing chant from the massed rows of mourners as the body of Oscar Thornton (in a flower-draped casket atop the wooden pyramid) was devoured in furnace heat. The funeral ceremony would have seemed barbarous to an Occidental; in Muong Toa, it was part of tradition.

"Was my speech overdone?" Chan asked.

He had spoken for a solid hour before the match touched the pyre. Indra, standing at John's side in the first row of mourners, had whispered a running translation—and Lex Wilde, taking busy notes behind them, had added his own approving murmur. Regardless of its bombast, John knew the eulogy had struck the proper note. From Chan's first outburst, the crowd that choked the hillside (dressed in the dead-white garments that symbolize death in the Orient) had responded with a single voice.

"It *was* too long," said Chan. "And much too florid. These are simple people. They'd have felt cheated if I'd talked a moment less."

The younger Thornton's candor had served to clear John's brain of sentiment. It was true the Valley people demanded that a funeral be noisy—if only to register the protest of the loved ones who remained in earthly toils. Had Chan failed to shout out his grief, they would have felt sure his father was unhappy in the other world.

"I don't have to tell *you* his death was a deliverance," said Chan. "He always prayed he'd go quietly. I think he was ready to go, after that last talk with us."

"Death always makes a doctor feel unwanted. You've conquered that feeling. I'll try to do likewise."

"Life's a continuing process, John. Our best tribute to Father's memory is to carry on."

"In Muong Toa, or the lab?"

"Why not in both?"

"Dud Porter may have a new approach when he arrives from Chiang Mai."

"I'm glad he's bringing in a jet burner. It may break a few of our roadblocks."

72

"Don't pin too many hopes on Dud," John said carefully. "He may live up to his nickname."

"You'd never have brought him here if you didn't expect results."

The microbiologist shook off his friend's persistence, not too amiably. "Stop behaving like Lex Wilde. Dud's a genius in his field but we can't expect him to pass a miracle."

"Did you know that Wilde plans to fly out with Indra?"

"He told me while the funeral was still in progress." Lex had already announced that the story he would be filing on Oscar Thornton's obsequies would be a major effort. He had even managed to take sub-rosa pictures with a watch-size camera—risking the well-known rage of primitive folk, who believe a camera robs them of their souls. At Chiang Mai, there were facilities for the transmission of photographs by radio.

"In a way," said Chan, "I suppose we owe today's ceremony to the world."

"Lex will do a good job," said John. "Pageantry is his stock in trade. Did he tell you he hopes to return?"

"With Dr. Porter, if possible," said Chan dourly. "He'll arrange his own transport later, if Indra can't wait. I've many good friends in Thailand. If you wish, they'll refuse him re-entry."

"We can't do that, Chan. Lex and I made a bargain."

The younger Thornton moved to the clinic window to study activities on the airstrip. The Dakota had just been wheeled from its hangar. Indra, already in her coveralls, was checking the fuel pumps with a mechanic.

"We'll leave things on that basis, since you insist," said Chan. "Speaking of Dr. Porter, are you still planning to meet him in Chiang Mai?"

"If it won't interfere with our schedule."

"I was hoping you'd stay with the convertor this afternoon. There's another cholera flare-up on the mountain. I should look into it."

"In that case, I'll be glad to remain."

Chan put a hand on John's arm. "I might as well admit I was testing you. Now that Father's gone, I've been mortally

73

afraid you'd take off. After all, we've picked each other's brains for several days with damned poor results."

"I promised your father I'd stay, and I'm keeping that promise. At least until I'm sure that solar conversion has failed us completely."

"I'd never hold you to your promise—not if you feel I've given you all I can on this project. You can take a few vials of the mutation and head for your own bailiwick."

"You *created* that mutation, Chan. D'you think I'd steal it?"

"Keep your temper, John. As I say, I'm only testing. Then it's still all for one and one for all?"

When John found himself joining in Chan's laughter, he knew they were friends again. Dumas had been their boyhood favorite, *The Three Musketeers* a book they had prized above all others.

"Now Dud's en route," he said, "we can *really* be Athos, Porthos and Aramis. This time, we'll promote Indra to d'Artagnan. She was always the best fencer of the lot."

After the discussion in the clinic, Chan had gone to the hospital garage to tune up a Land Rover for his trip to the hills: the dictum that life must go on at Muong Toa, John saw, would be applied literally. The visit with Oscar Thornton's heir had left him curiously empty, despite its warm finale. He was still fighting a nameless depression when he walked into the glare of afternoon, to speed the Dakota on its way.

Lex Wilde had just emerged from the guest bungalow, with his portable slung on one shoulder.

"You're looking rather solemn, John."

"Doesn't the occasion demand it?"

"There's no need to bear down, now the eulogies are on file. How did your talk with young Thornton go?"

"You promised to stop asking direct questions. Remember?"

"All I'm asking is where I stand here. If I risk going outside, will he let me back?"

"You aren't exactly *persona grata,* Lex. Chan was all for

74

refusing you an entry permit. He could make it stick in Chiang Mai."

"Meaning that you *do* have a guilty secret behind those padlocks?"

"Not at all. My friend finds it harder than I to adjust to your presence."

"So do most dictators," said the journalist. "I'll take that as a compliment."

"In your place, I'd keep such opinions to myself. I've persuaded him to let you return—if you'll provide your own transport."

"My paper is arranging that now. I'm making a trip to Bangkok before I head north again. Can you do without my company for a few days?"

"You needn't come back at all, Lex. If we have a newsbreak here, I'll keep it exclusive."

"There's no substitute for spot reporting. When that lab takes down its padlocks, I want to describe the event firsthand. Just as I'm describing today's *suttee*."

"It wasn't a *suttee*, as you're well aware."

"They burned the patriarch, didn't they? Just as they burned Gandhi?"

"Use the word, if you insist," said John resignedly. "You can also pretend Chan and I are old-fashioned alchemists, if it makes you happier. We'll never live up to the image, I assure you."

"Suppose the break comes while I'm away? Will you keep it on ice, as you promised?"

"We've already arranged that. All I ask is this. If you do return, don't outstay your welcome."

"We can agree on that item too," said Wilde. "Next Friday, the President's addressing the NATO meeting in Paris: I must cover him in person. It gives you five more days to produce the story you guaranteed." With a resounding slap on John's shoulder, the journalist loped toward the open door of the plane. The fuselage trembled while he settled his bulk in the rear seat. Almost at once, he began typing, at machine-gun speed.

Moving carefully away from the door, John waved to Indra, who was approaching from the hangar.

"You'll need a coat when we're airborne," she said.

"Mr. Wilde will be your escort this trip."

The girl's eyebrows lifted. "Only yesterday you said you couldn't wait to confer with your assistant."

"Dudley was well briefed in my radiogram. I'll trust you to deliver him safely."

"Why did you change your mind?"

"Chan changed it for me. He has cholera cases in the hills. Someone must stay with our friend the octopus, while it digests a new batch of culture."

"Did he say *cholera* again?"

"He's a doctor too, you know."

Indra stepped into the shadow of a wing-tip, well away from the open cockpit door.

"You've been here almost a week, John, and you've slaved like a Trojan. Haven't you considered rebelling?"

"We mentioned that the day the convertor backfired. Do you recall my answer?"

"Sometimes I think you're too good to be true. In your place, I'd have given up long ago."

"Strangely enough, Chan suggested I do just that—now I've picked his brains."

"Did he think for a moment you'd accept?"

"Did *you*, Indra?"

The girl's hand had fallen on his arm. When he turned to go—if only to test her mood—he felt the fingers tighten.

"Dr. Porter—and the equipment he's bringing. They're our *dernières cartouches,* aren't they?"

"The last shots in the locker," John agreed quietly. "If they fail, Dud and I will be en route to San Francisco in a few days' time." He breathed deep, then spoke the thought closest to his heart. "You'll join us, Indra—if you'll face the facts."

Indra made no attempt to pick up the dare. Instead, she left the shadow of the wing to dismiss the mechanics, who had already removed the chocks from the wheels.

"Wasn't *success* the price of my departure—day before yesterday?"

"The picture's changed, now that Papa Oscar's no longer with us. Can you deny it?"

"Finish the thought, John. I haven't disagreed—so far."

"You've seen Chan take over authority here, without breaking stride. It's a privilege he won't share. Win or lose, he'll stay true to form when we've closed up shop."

"Even if I leave with you?"

"Chan won't keep you a captive princess forever. It's the Chlorella equation he wants, not your love."

"Aren't you being rather harsh?"

"I think not. Today, for the first time, I've seen Chan Thornton clearly. Believe me, he doesn't need you, or anyone. Fame is the only spur he answers."

Indra moved back to the plane. Expecting a flaming denial, John felt his spirits bound as she turned away to test a strut that needed no attention from the pilot.

"You could be wrong, John—"

"For Chan's sake, I almost hope I am."

"Until we're sure, let's try to be fair—to us all."

In the shelter of the cockpit door, she held out her arms. The incessant chatter of Lex Wilde's Olivetti was assurance that the journalist would not observe their quick, half-guilty embrace. The kiss they had shared in the lab had been wildly impromptu, a thanksgiving at John's escape from death. Today's was a pledge of love.

Forcing himself to turn back to the laboratory before the plane had vanished in the mountain gap to the south, John found that Chan had left only a single technician in charge that afternoon.

The man had been assigned to watch over the convertor, cut to half-speed as it always was in the doctors' absence. Originally the younger Thornton had agreed that the *bat jhow yee* had earned a rest, after its near-death from methane poisoning. Later he had countermanded his own order, insisted on a complete repair of the plastic tubing, and laid out a series of comparison runs with original *Chlorella Thorntoni* cultures.

Moving automatically, John stepped up the tempo of the

main pump and made his now-familiar notations on the delivery from the centrifuge, as it separated mature cells from the liquid medium that had nourished them. When a full batch had received its maximum dehydration from this agency, he removed the trays from the powerful, whirling arms and carried them to the outside oven. Thanks to long hours in his own lab, he could anticipate the results of that yield, without recourse to his current work-sheet. When the last tray had gone to its drying-rack, he asked his helper to bring Chan's dossier to the worktable, then dismissed him for the day.

The reports, covering test runs of many months' duration, occupied a dozen notebooks: it was his first opportunity to go through the record *in toto*. As he had expected, the entries were meticulous: despite the marginal comments and the closely-written footnotes (both largely in Chinese), John found he could translate without difficulty. It was an absorbing glimpse into the mind of a fellow scientist, even though it told him little that was new.

Chan, he perceived, had pushed through a score of harvestings with almost identical results. Throughout, he had shown the dogged persistence of the researcher. The first notes on the discovery of the mutation, the mysterious explosion of the growth-rate and its tendency to devour its own achievement, were set down in the same fashion. There was no hint of the angry mind behind them, or the frustration that would have driven most men to admit defeat.

A new page (with a Chinese heading John could not decipher) told a different—and at first glance, puzzling—story. Late in the previous year, it was evident that Chan had run an experiment in nutrition, using a rigid control-system and employing the inhabitants of two Meo villages as human guinea pigs. The notes had been summarized from several hundred work-sheets. In one village, a quantity of dried algae had been the main source of nourishment. In the other, the eternal Asian rice had been the staple. In both tests, the amounts of these basic foods had been held to the minimum necessary to sustain life.

There had been no question of the results. Despite the low-calorie allotment, the eaters of dried algae had turned in a near-perfect health record. The rice eaters had produced the expected cases of beriberi (that bellwether of all vitamin-lack diseases) plus eye ailments and occasional disorders of the joints.

John closed the book after a long perusal and restored it to its shelf. Despite the chilling impersonality of those entries, he could understand the compulsion that had driven Chan to make his test. The fact that he could persuade the intransigent Meo to serve as his agents spoke well for his authority. There was also the alarming suggestion that these nomadic people (suspicious, as always, of the lowlands) had refused to make use of the cooperative farms Papa Oscar had established long ago, as a vital element in the Valley's well-being.

A warning blinker, reminding the microbiologist that the drying process was completed, broke in on his musings. Lifting the still-hot trays from their racks, he carried them to the scale. Once again, he found, the figures were more impressive than conclusive. Thanks to Muong Toa's abundant sunlight, Chan's harvest had been consistently high. It was still only a laboratory demonstration—and still far too costly per kilogram to solve the world's need for a cheap, all-purpose food.

The nutrition test, John added, was a dramatic footnote that actually proved nothing. The harvest of his own subspecies had been a dietary triumph, but an economic failure. Its mutation, for all its virtuoso qualities, remained a sport of biology, a maverick that was valueless on both counts until its rebel nature could be broken.

The drone of a plane motor, catching John with a slide rule still in his hand, was a startling reminder of the passage of time. Absorbed in Chan's notebooks (and the fascinating speculations they had aroused), he could not quite believe the Dakota had returned from Chiang Mai.

There was still time to charge the convertor with a fresh test run and set the pump at half-speed, before the plane roared in for its landing.

Ten minutes later, when he unlocked the laboratory door

and stood there to welcome his assistant, John saw that Indra
had followed the Dakota to its hangar—leaving a pair of
houseboys to transport the small mountain of equipment on
the airstrip. For once, he was glad she had held aloof.
Watching from the doorframe, he was sure his assistant would
not stir from the tarmac until the last item was loaded in the
waiting truck. Only when that chore was behind him did Dr.
Dudley Porter turn toward the low-eaved laboratory building, with the instinct of a homing pigeon.

Returning Dud's cheery wave (made as casually as though
they had parted yesterday), John reflected that few men fitted
their picture frames more accurately than his chief technician.
He had known statesmen who resembled clerks, poets who
could have passed for fullbacks, a world-famous nuclear
physicist whose baby-faced stare suggested a happy moron.
Even today (riding the fender of a pickup truck in southeast
Asia) Dud was marked for his profession. He was deceptively
slight of frame, round-shouldered from the microscope; his
thin fox-face was pale from indoor midnights. One needed
a second look to realize the slender body was wiry as a
coiled spring, that the eyes behind those dark horn-rims were
completely alert.

"Man, this is the most," said Dud, and bounced from the
truck to shake hands. (An occasional trial run of jive talk
was one of his few concessions to his century.)

"I'm glad you endorse Muong Toa, Dr. Porter."

"A far-out paradise, Boss. And I'll give you Bardot for my
pilot, any day. When do I get to know her better?"

"Did you think I brought you here for a vacation? Let's
help these boys unload."

"Like you see, I got you a jet burner. A friend of mine at
Lockheed came through nobly. What do we use for fuel?"

"I'll show you later. Along with some other things you'll
find hard to believe." John led the way through the vestibule.
Already he had the sensation of burdens lifting. It was like
Dud Porter to leap at once to concrete problems.

"I sensed a cryptic quality in your cable," said the assistant.
"You'll find me hard to surprise."

"You may eat those words in the next hour."

80

Like every worker in Chan Thornton's compound, the two houseboys knew their job. Dud Porter, standing with a copy of his bill of lading, checked each case as it went into the laboratory stores. His jet burner (whose several parts made up the most bulky items) was saved for last. At John's order, the houseboys retired from the scene, leaving its handling to the microbiologist and his chief helper.

"We'll install this later," said John. "Let's carry it to the outer court for now. You can work out its attachment to the convertor."

Dud did not speak when John slid back the panels to expose Chan's octopus. Instead, he moved round the monster admiringly, checking each item of its construction, and testing its complex of plastic tubes with a series of expert palpations that were almost caresses.

"What's its conversion percentage?"

"Better than twenty percent."

"As against one or two percent in most field plants. No question about it, we're going to put the farmers out of business."

"Not at a production cost of fifty cents a kilo."

"We'll lick those figures, too. How much solar energy can you count on in these parts—compared to Frisco?"

"Nearly ten times as much."

"That means we'll need God's own amount of $CO_2$. Where do we get it?"

"I'll answer that with Exhibit A. Sit down at the microscope table."

John needed only a moment to prepare a hanging drop of his subspecies. While Dudley studied it, he prepared a second, using a culture of Chan's X-ray mutation. His assistant was still staring at the first slide when he returned to the table.

"How did our child get into this nursery, Boss?"

"It threw me too, for a moment, but the answer's simple. We made the culture available months ago."

"I'd still call it fast traveling."

"Not for Dr. Chan Thornton—and the trust fund he draws on in Texas."

"Why didn't he ask us for it direct?"

"This is his favorite form of surprise," John said dryly, and slipped the mutation slide beneath the lenses. "Take a look at Exhibit B."

The assistant bent over the oculars, and John saw the stooped shoulders tense abruptly. Several moments passed before Dud looked up. The eyes behind the horn-rims were slightly glazed.

"Like crazy," he said softly. "Like nothing else but *crazy*. What tissue is this from? Don't tell me it's a blood culture from your patient."

"Oscar Thornton died of malignant leukemia. But even at the end, the lymphocytes in his blood resembled lymphocytes."

"These Johnny-jump-ups look like nothing ever created, in heaven or on earth. I can't even recognize the tissue they came from."

"There's good reason. That subspecies didn't come from a tissue. Originally is was *Chlorella Thorntoni*."

Dud shook his head dazedly. "Come down from Cloud Nine. I'm too bushed right now to join you."

"It's still our child, Dud. With a new feature added—a little X ray."

"A mutation!"

"You've finally named it," said John. "Basically it represents the type of runaway that causes cancer. Since this is simple cell division, the same laws don't apply."

"How did the mutation happen?"

"By accident—like so many discoveries of this kind."

"Apparently your friend has licked the problem of growth-rate."

"He's gone a long way."

"It's a *food* bomb, Boss. A gasser to end all gassers. The biggest thing since our boys cracked the atom."

"Take another look at that microscope. You've seen the beginning, not the ending."

Dudley Porter studied the slide for a long time. Watching his absolute concentration, John could almost hear the wheels turn behind that pale forehead.

"It's more than a food bomb," he said at last. "It's a methane factory too."

"That's our *bête noire*, Dud. Can we handle it?"

"No wonder you wanted a jet burner."

"The way I see it, this mutation—in quantity—grows so fast we could never supply it with carbon dioxide and nutrition. Not in its present state, at least. Without them, it's bound to degenerate and form methane."

"What's the cure, Boss?"

"We must remove the methane from the tubes *before* it causes clogging. I'm hoping we can pipe it into that jet burner to help us burn our extra waste. That way, we'll solve two problems: the cells will have room to work out their life cycle, and we'll produce extra $CO_2$ to help them along."

"It makes sense, John. The idea of burning waste is right on the ball. Is it yours?"

"That was Chan's thinking. Do you approve?"

"It's far out—but not too far out to handle. Piping that methane to the furnace should close the deal. It'll take doing, of course: there's bound to be trial and error. Can your friend stand the gaff?"

"He's a scientist too, Dud. I've evidence he's a patient one."

"He may need that patience."

"Did you bring enough tubing?"

"All you can possibly use—like you said in your wireless." Dud stepped under the skylight and studied the nest of solar exposures in the court. "I'll get on the job at once: it's going to take a lot of leeches." He circled the alcove another time, probing each corner with eyes that missed nothing, writing a phantom calculation with a flick of his fingers. It was a signal John knew well—proof that the task at hand had banished all else from his assistant's mind.

"Stay with it, Dud," he said. "I'll finish stowing your airfreight."

"Incidentally, Boss, I brought some cultures of *Thorntoni* from our incubators. They should be incubated again, pronto. They've been chilled for quite a while."

The algae incubator stood against the far wall of the lab.

Knowing his presence in the alcove was no longer needed, John picked up the rack of culture tubes, crossed to the heavy door, and turned the key. Chan had usually mixed the nutrient for the test runs, and added the desired culture. Before he added Dud's vials to the incubator, John studied its contents carefully, to make sure each rack was labeled. Chan's mutation, as he had expected, occupied a place of honor, at eye level: conventional cultures of his own subspecies stood on the shelf above. At first glance, they seemed replicas of the containers in his hand.

About to add the new vials to the shelf, John leaned closer to read their labels—and recoiled sharply from what he saw. A second, closer look confirmed his first impression.

There were perhaps a dozen racks of *Chlorella Thorntoni* on the shelf, and all of them bore Chan's name on neatly typed address cards. It was the labels on the tubes themselves that had struck him like a blow. At the top of each tube was a dragon-shaped insignia, bearing the stamp of a laboratory in Shanghai. Below, a printed legend stated that the culture's point of origin was John's own Nutrition Foundation in San Francisco.

The microbiologist stood for a long time with his eyes fixed on the rack. Part of his brain was racing ahead to pin down the meaning of those rampant dragons. The rest of his mind (the part that preferred sentiment to reason) was searching for an explanation that continued to elude him.

When he closed the incubator door and turned back to the alcove, where Dud Porter was crouched over the still-dismembered jet burner, he had controlled his agitation.

"Stop playing house, Dud," he said. "We'll begin work in the morning."

"What's bugging you now, John?"

"We're taking a ride before dinner. You can use the fresh air."

"Someone must stay with the convertor."

"It's safe to set the pump at half-speed. Dr. Thornton will check it tonight."

"Judging by his workshop, he's a man after my own heart." Dud abandoned his tentative assembly of the jet

84

burner and left the alcove on lagging feet. "Do I *have* to be a tourist, Boss? I've already seen the country from the air."

"Aren't you curious about Muong Toa?"

"Thanks to you, I've visited most corners of this small planet. The more I see of natives, the more they look the same." Dud cast a last, regretful look at the *bat jhow yee* and picked up a Calcutta helmet much the worse for wear. "Where does the tour begin?"

"Since you prefer algae to humans, I won't insist on formal sightseeing." John collected his thoughts: he was sharply conscious that he had been speaking at random. "Dr. Thornton is making sick calls in the mountains. I thought we might meet him halfway."

"Do we walk, or does this kampong provide transport?"

"We'll go by Land Rover. I want you to drive so you'll remember the road."

In the hospital garage, he took the seat beside Dudley Porter in the Rover. He had decided to take the monastery road, since he had no real wish to meet Chan en route. The discovery of the containers had raised questions that cried out for answers. His instincts told him that the presence of his assistant would slow his urge toward drastic action. So would Prince Ngo Singh, if his advice was available at this hour.

Halfway to the temple gate, John remembered this was the time of evening prayer, when all visitors were excluded. Until the stroke of six, even the outer court would be off limits. At his request, Dud swung the Rover to the shoulder of the road, to park the sturdy vehicle in a mimosa thicket. The maneuver concealed their presence completely, though it gave them a sweeping view of the valley, including the track that entered the jungle screen below the Gates of Hell.

"Aren't you feeling well, Boss?"

Facing his assistant across the wheel, John wondered how much of his thinking he dared put into words.

"Do I look ill?"

"If you want it straight, I'd say you were fighting a tempertantrum. Maybe you'd better let off steam before you blow your stack."

"Actually, it's the reason I brought you here."

"Does this job have bugs you didn't mention?"

"There may be bugs *outside* the lab. Had you thought of that angle?"

"Meaning the food bomb and international relations?"

"Doesn't it give you second thoughts, Dud?"

"Like who feeds whom?"

"You'd admit it's a poser—in any language?"

"It's Washington's headache, not ours."

"Suppose we come up with a solution to the problem—and it gets into the wrong hands?"

"Suppose the wrong man triggers a megaton tomorrow?"

"If that's in the stars, you go under," John said quietly. "Can you sleep on the prospect?"

"Like a babe-in-arms," said Dud. "It's the reason seconal was invented. To say nothing of bourbon and freewheeling sex—" He broke off as the microbiologist held up a hand for silence. The throb of a car motor had reached them from the jungle-choked trail below.

"That will be Chan," said John.

"Shouldn't we coast downhill and greet him?"

"Introductions can come later. Right now, we're about to indulge in a bit of spying."

The second Land Rover had just lumbered into view. Reaching for the binoculars in the door-pocket of his own vehicle, John brought the trail below into focus. In that powerful lens, the car below them (a mere crawling ant in the greenery) seemed near enough to touch.

Chan was at the wheel. A single passenger sat beside him, a Chinese in a dusty workman's smock, his splinted arm resting on the car door. The back seats of the Rover were stacked with crates, lashed down under a flapping tarpaulin. It was odd (thought John) that a broken grommet, releasing a corner of that coverall, should provide the clue he sought. He handed the binoculars to his assistant.

"Can you read the name on that bottom carton?"

"Of course. Quinacrine hydrochloride, a standard medication in the tropics."

"And the stamp above it?"

"It's Eastern lingo. Don't quote me, but I'd guess it was Chinese."

"Dr. Thornton's passenger is a casualty from a construction job in Yunnan. If *he* crossed the border this afternoon, those drug cartons did likewise."

"What's your point?"

"Why should Muong Toa import drugs from China, when it has airfreight service from Thailand?"

"You say your friend brings in traction patients. Isn't it natural to bring a few cases of atabrine on the same haul?"

Anticipating this dismissal, John realized he must open his mind completely. Dud sat in dutiful silence while he recited the facts of a week in Muong Toa, beginning with the polyglot complexion of Chan Thornton's ward. It was a relief to describe the strange nutrition-test he had unearthed from Chan's ledger, the algal cultures in the incubator that had matched Dud's own supply from San Francisco—and finally, the proof Dud himself had witnessed, that the hospital was importing medicines from Yunnan.

His assistant's face did not change during the recital. Once he polished his horn-rims and stared at the valley floor, where only a dust plume marked the passage of the Rover.

"Is that the bill of particulars, John?"

"Isn't it enough?"

"In your place, I'd relax. Unless, of course, you can prove your friend's a card-carrying member of the Party."

"Obviously, he's nothing of the sort. It's just as obvious he's established a *modus vivendi*."

"He told you that much, the day you got here. Isn't it natural he'd open his ward to a Chinese construction camp—as an act of mercy?"

"How d'you explain those damned culture tubes?"

"Your subspecies has been in use for quite a while, John. Remember a fellow named Sung, at the Foundation last year? An exchange scholar from Taiwan?"

"He was a first-rate biochemist."

"When Dr. Sung left San Francisco, a dozen cases of your culture medium went with him. I've since heard he defected to the mainland. He *must* have used your Chlorella as part

87

of his procedure, and found it useful. Eventually he'd be bound to order more of the same—"

"He couldn't buy it in the States."

"He might, via Canada. They sell wheat to Peiping: they may be selling biologicals too, for all we know. He could also have ordered his supplies from Tokyo or Calcutta. So could your friend Thornton. In his place, I'd get materials by the shortest haul."

"So my suspicions are unjustified?"

"Sleep on them: you'll see how right I am."

John glanced at his wristwatch, saw it was nearly six, and turned the ignition key.

"Oddly enough, that's just what I mean to do. Drive me to the monastery, please. And keep memorizing the trail; you'll be going back alone."

Dud did not reopen the subject until he had swung the car into the narrow turnaround before the temple gate.

"Shall I park here and wait?"

"Send back for me in the morning. I'm spending the night, as the Prince's guest."

The assistant stared doubtfully at the massive walls. The outer gate had just been opened, to admit a sound of chanting from the great hall. It was a time of meditation, open to monks and penitents alike.

"Are you about to go Zen?" he asked. "You must be *really* bugged."

"I'm only an overnight pilgrim, Dud."

"Do they take paying guests here, just like a motel?"

"The comparison isn't too farfetched," said John. "The road-weary traveler makes his contribution in advance, chooses a meditation cell, and sleeps until sunrise. Let's hope I'll be as lucky."

"You're still worried, aren't you? My alleged opinions didn't help at all."

"Let's say they cleared my head."

"Boss, we're a pair of researchers with a job to finish. Let's get with it."

"Tomorrow will do, Dud."

"Can I make a start while I wait for you?"

"Set up the jet burner, by all means. If you have time, you can connect the tapping tubes."

Dud let out his breath in a happy sigh. "That means a full night's work. Can I fire up?"

"Cut that corner, if you like. Just don't start a new run until I'm on hand."

"What shall I tell Dr. Thornton?"

"Say the actual process is in my head. I'm stealing tonight to mull it over."

"Suppose he doesn't believe me?"

"He'll have to, Dud. In the circumstances, I've earned a touch of mystery too."

Fearing that his khaki work clothes might strike an alien note, John had kept clear of evening prayers when he entered the courtyard. In the time of meditation that followed, he had waited patiently in the cell he had chosen (a cubicle carved from the inner side of the monastery wall). While he ate the modest supper the monks shared with their pilgrims, he had watched a brief rainsquall drench the mountain defiles and fade into streamers of mist in the teak forests on the lower slopes.

He was counting the first stars (and feeling his spirits rejuvenate with each breath of this tranquil air) when a figure approached his cell door. Even in the wan light, John sensed it was a visitor like himself—a tall young man whose patrician bearing seemed at complete variance with his peasant garb.

"The Chao Kueng will join you shortly, Doctor. Please wait for him in the courtyard."

Expecting the summons, John was not too startled at the means the Prince had used to convey it. Obviously his messenger was either a relative or a lieutenant, who, for the best of reasons in these troubled times, chose to travel incognito. Usage demanded that he respect the disguise, so he did not rise from his seat on the doorsill of the cell—contenting himself with a word of acceptance as the visitor continued on his way, to take the path to the valley.

Protocol also demanded that John go at once to the bench

beside the fountain. When Ngo Singh sat down beside him in the growing dark, he had already surrendered to the conviction that time had lost its meaning—that their discussion would resume, without strain, from its last interruption.

"I am told you plan to spend the night," said the Prince. "Does this mean you've brought a new dilemma to our door?"

"Call it a new look at the same problem, Your Highness. This time, perhaps, I can solve it alone."

"If you prefer, I will be an attentive ear in the dark."

"Can you spare a half-hour?"

"Of course, Dr. Merchant. Self-communion can be a lonely business to a man like yourself, who demands absolute answers."

"Next time I come here, I'll send a word in advance. I fear I broke in on your own affairs tonight."

"The man who summoned you was one of my sons. In happier times, he was known as Prince Fa Ngoum—after the king who united this area over six centuries ago, as the Land of a Million Elephants. Now he goes by the name of Goum and works for his bread on a farm beyond South Mountain."

"Does he bring news often from the world?"

"When he can spare the time. Tomorrow he takes the north trail to work awhile in Yunnan. Yes, Doctor, you could call Ngoum a useful informant. I have others, of course."

"If you could confide their reports, they might prove of value to me."

"Do your problems resemble mine? The thought is flattering."

"Like yours, they are concerned with war and peace. Does your son believe strife will come to the Valley?"

"Not if we do nothing to provoke the devils beyond the Gates."

"Your situation remains unchanged, then?"

The Prince hesitated before he spoke. "When you were last here, I mentioned invaders who had their day and departed."

"Then you do fear a new onslaught?"

"As I say, there is no present cause for alarm. I may feel otherwise, after my son has made his journey north."

"Is he going to seek work on the power dam?"

"Such is his intention. We have heard fantastic rumors of that construction. So far, I trust none of the witnesses who have reported here. My son will bring back the true answer."

"Last time, you felt you could trust Chan Thornton's judgment."

"I thought him sincere when he said you could conduct your experiment in peace. And that the Enchanted Valley would shelter you, while you took the risk—"

"Then there is a risk involved?"

The Prince smiled in the fast-growing dusk.

"To your future renown, perhaps—if the experiment fulfills its promise. The mutation of *Chlorella Thorntoni* would bear your friend's name. Apparently you've resigned yourself to that prospect."

"The major discovery is his, not mine. Tonight I have greater cause for concern. It may be only fancy, but I can't rest until I state it."

The Prince's sublime poise—while John repeated his discoveries—was wonderfully soothing.

"So far, Doctor—if I understand you correctly—your fears are only of the mind."

"Surely I've cause for concern."

"Are those fears in your heart as well?"

"It's a question I can't answer. That's why I sought refuge here."

"This noon you could have flown back to Chiang Mai. Tomorrow you could have been in Bangkok, boarding a plane for home. Instead, you have permitted your assistant to join you here. Before morning he will be ready to reactivate the solar convertor. Doesn't this mean you still believe in Chan?"

"I'm trying hard, Your Highness."

"Let us assume the experiment fulfills your hopes. This food bomb, as you call it, might stop an Asian war. Postponed a year, it could be too late."

"You advise me to continue—is that it?"

"I'm hoping you'll compare unproved doubts with what

91

you know. Perhaps you'll find that Chan Thornton has done no more than buy immunity for the Valley."

"Even if that's true, I don't envy him his choice."

"I, too, have faced the same problem here," said the Prince. "Don't judge us too harshly, if we yield a point at times, in order to keep our independence."

"I won't deny Chan seems his own man."

"He told you the truth about his ward patients. His notes were open to your inspection. So were those tubes in his incubator. Why not ask *him* how they reached Muong Toa?"

"I have that answer now. The labels prove they came from Shanghai."

"Does that mean your friend himself is evil—because he gives and takes help where he can find it? Do you insist that all your values must be black and white? To the Oriental mind, Chinese Communism is a disease that will run its course. Chan Thornton, like his father, has managed to live with it and avoid it."

"That sounds like a tall order, Prince Singh."

"For many years this valley has produced more food than it needs. Even in old Dr. Thornton's day, rice sacks were carried into Yunnan on the backs of coolies. Chan has continued the bounty."

"In the States, we'd call that a shakedown to a gangster."

"Here, it means that men dying of hunger can exist a little longer. Meanwhile, our small rice bowl has been left to its own devices." The Prince pondered his next remark. "As a scientist, you must be familiar with a Chinese called T. K. Yu."

"I've studied his writings. He's one of the great names in agronomy."

"Dr. Yu has been working in Yunnan for two years, doing his best to improve the rice yield. He's brought in a corps of doctors—and several hospital planes—to work on diet problems. He's flown to Muong Toa more than once, to compare notes with Chan. Last spring, a chemical compound they'd been using here was introduced in Chinese paddies, with good effect. In Chan's place, would you have withheld such help?"

"My country's given similar aid—through the World Health Organization."

"So it has, Dr. Merchant. Please forgive me. Somehow I can't visualize those United Nations groups too clearly. Perhaps it's their resounding names."

"I suppose it's only natural that one scientist should visit another, in these circumstances. I've no intention of sharing our food bomb with Dr. Yu, regardless of his motives."

"Your attitude is understandable," said the Prince. "So far, I fail to see the basis for your fears. This algal mutation is Chan's secret—and yours. If you can harness it, you have every right to dictate its use. Do you believe that Chan would reveal it to Dr. Yu—or to anyone—without your consent?"

"We can't keep such a discovery to ourselves forever."

"True. Your food bomb, like the H-bomb, must belong to the world someday. Then, of course, you can return to the realm of pure science, and resign the problem of its use to others."

"Meanwhile, I'm to trust my oldest friend. Is that what you're saying?"

"A week ago, Dr. Merchant, you crossed our borders hoping to save a man who was your second father. You also hoped to persuade Indra Lal to return with you. Now, I gather, you feel that Chan stands between you. Could that be why you've tried to make him a villain?"

"I can't believe I'd be that unjust, sir."

"Perhaps your feeling goes deeper. As an American, you may think all Asians should be distrusted. Especially when you hold this great a secret in your hand."

"Suppose I stay on until we've finished our experiment. Will that prove I'm not just another isolationist, but a citizen of the world?"

"It will do more. It will show that East and West can think as one, when the salvation of mankind is the goal. To me, that is the real breakthrough all of us are seeking."

"These are large thoughts to sleep on, Your Highness."

Ngo Singh rose from the bench. His hand rested briefly

on John's shoulder, in a familiar gesture of benediction. When he turned to go, he laid a small pillbox on the bench.

"You need rest tonight, Doctor. May I reverse our roles, and prescribe a potion that cannot fail you?"

"Is it local or universal?"

The Prince smiled. "When you saved the Kha tribesman who got in the way of a poisoned spear, you found that the people of the hills grow many potent herbs. The contents of this box are harmless. But they will bring you sleep—and with it, perhaps, the peace of mind you seek."

The box, John discovered, contained a single yellow-green pellet. He swallowed the preparation without pausing for thought, and washed it down with a dipper of springwater. The taste was strongly herbal, the odor faintly acrid. Fifteen minutes later, when he had blown out his candle and stretched on the hard bunk in his cell, he had already begun to float between earth and heaven.

The sensation was odd, but not unpleasant. The opiate (he could hardly doubt this was a derivative of the poppy) seemed to detach him from reality completely—as though his body were receding, his spirit and his thoughts rising to some higher level from which he could view the scene below. He could no longer tell if he were asleep or awake when he found himself on a high mountain—surely the highest in the universe, since he could observe the whole earth from its crest.

Chan and Indra and Dudley Porter were beside him. It was part of the magic of his dream that the solar convertor was there as well—and that it loomed even higher than their mountaintop, its new jet burner in perfect tandem with its pulsating arms, its drying oven delivering the end product of the packed Chlorella cells in massive profusion. Then, as is the way of midnight visions, mountain and convertor became one, though the four workers continued to stand on its summit. In the valley below, people had gathered by the millions to partake of its endless harvest.

He could see these people clearly, their faces uplifted to the mountain and its life-giving flood. Brown faces, black faces, yellow and white, they were lighted with the same inner fire. This was a world made new, a happy cosmos where no man hated since no man hungered.

When he wakened, he was not surprised to find it already morning. Parts of the vision lingered: he could not remember when he had felt more rested, or more serene. Nor did it seem in the least strange, after he had entered the courtyard of the temple, to find Indra waiting at the gate, beneath the wheel of the Land Rover.

# 4.

JOHN hesitated in the shadow of the gate. Remembering that he had asked for transport, he had hoped the hospital would send a houseboy. The decision he had made overnight was a firm one, but he was not quite ready to repeat it to the girl he loved.

The pause, he told himself, was less than courageous. Lifting a hand in greeting, he walked into the bright spring sunlight, hoping the gesture seemed carefree.

"Have you been waiting long, Indra?"

"Less than five minutes."

This morning, to his surprise, he saw she was still wearing her denim coveralls, that her face was drawn from lack of sleep.

"I'm glad I was an early riser," he said cautiously.

"Chan asked me to bring you back."

"Where is he?"

"In the lab—where else? I've been working there myself since midnight."

The microbiologist slipped into the seat beside Indra and took her hand. The fingers were rigid, and they did not return his pressure.

"Don't judge me too harshly until you've heard me out," he said.

"No one begrudges you a night's rest, John."

"Dud promised to work straight through, if need be. I don't think we've lost any ground."

Indra put the Rover in low gear and took the first hazardous slope from the monastery gate.

"Dr. Porter says his new jet burner will help us enormously."

"Dud's an incurable optimist. He's also a magician with solar convertors."

"Chan's wild to test our first batch of mutation. Why did you give orders to wait?"

"I wanted to go over everything—before we put the test in motion."

"The changes in the convertor?" Indra asked. "Or the cure for your mental block?"

"Shall we say I've been working hard on both?"

"It isn't like you to be suspicious, John."

"And it isn't like you to speak of mental blocks."

"I'll be glad to explain—if you'll do the same."

"If this is a quarrel, you'd best begin it. What I have to tell you isn't too easy."

The girl swung the Rover into the shade of the mimosa thicket where Dud Porter had parked the preceding afternoon. Once again John had the sensation of an appointment with fate, a date as irreversible as birth or death.

"It seems I came in at this point," he said. "Are you aware of that?"

"Why else would I stop here? When you took off yesterday, I guessed you would meet Chan. Just to be sure, I went to the hospital roof. It wasn't hard to guess why you drove into this thicket."

John kept his eyes on the road below. Wondering how much Indra knew, he saw he could not put the question directly.

"I'd been wondering why Chan spent so much time in the mountains," he said at last.

"Do you think it was honest to *spy*?"

"It wasn't a happy choice, Indra. Yesterday, it seemed a shortcut to knowledge I needed badly."

"When did you first decide he'd gone over to the enemy?"

The girl sat unstirring while John recounted the story of his findings in the laboratory incubator.

"Wouldn't it have been simpler to come to me?"

"It didn't seem fair. Not when you'd refused to make a choice between us."

"I told you whom I'd choose, if I were a free agent."

"I'm sorry, Indra. The Prince seemed a better source of truth." It was time for his own attack, and John made it with regret. "I wish you'd told me *something* of what I . . . discovered on my own. You must have realized I'd be bowled over when I stumbled on those containers."

"I hoped you'd never find them," Indra said quickly. "So did Chan."

"Then this *was* a conspiracy to keep me in the dark?"

"I confess it freely. You must see why now."

"I've begun to, thanks to the Prince."

"Decisions of this sort are simpler in the States, John. *There,* you'd be free to call Chan a traitor, because he dared to feed the enemy's peasants. It's another story in a corner of Asia that has no real boundaries. Hunger is hunger here, no matter what tongue it speaks. We've always heeded its cry at Muong Toa."

"So this valley sends rice to Yunnan: that's common humanity. Suppose we control the mutation next month, and there's another hunger cry from that quarter? Would Chan donate our findings?"

"Not if you vetoed such help."

"He's an absolute ruler here. Why should he consult me—if the process is established, and I'm back in San Francisco?"

"He'll respect your wishes in this matter, John. I have his promise."

"When did you obtain it?"

"This morning, before I came to fetch you. The mutation's under padlock at this moment. Its use is a secret we've all sworn to keep. All that matters this morning is that we're on the edge of great things."

"I can see Dud Porter's infected you with his enthusiasm."

"He thinks we'll have a workable technique in a week. Or even sooner, if we solve the methane problem today."

"Dud could be right, of course."

"Haven't you *some* hope left?"

With an effort, John kept his voice cool: it was hard to resist the plea in the girl's eyes.

"I'll make no predictions at this time. To my mind, the important thing right now is that you and I understand each other."

"I *said* Chan would do as you wished. He gave his promise. If you have doubts, you'd better voice them."

"Don't put words in my mouth, Indra. My point's a simple one. Chan's been king here for a long time. Kings have their crotchets."

"You'll talk with him now?"

"At once."

"He's waiting in the clinic office. Shall we go to him together?"

"We'd best talk alone," John said. "I'd like you to join Dud at the convertor. He'll need assistance there."

"Does this mean you'll go on with the tests?"

"It's too late to stop the first run. Give me a half-hour with the monarch of Muong Toa. I hope we'll still be friends when we join you."

Chan paced the clinic office for a silent moment. His eyes were on the window when he spoke again.

"I'm glad I could restore your sense of proportion, John. I'm still a trifle shocked that you—shall I say, harbored such doubts?"

"You'll admit I had reason?"

"You could have brought your suspicions to me when I returned yesterday. There was no need to take them to the mountain."

"Why didn't you tell me you'd been accepting drugs and cultures from China—to settle hospital fees?"

"It never occurred to me an explanation was needed. Barter

98

payments of that sort are common on every border from here to Arabia. I'd forgotten how long you'd been away."

So far, John had felt no need to stir from the ancient horsehair couch, a spot he had occupied from old habit when his discussion with Chan began. It was the seat he had taken when he first met Papa Oscar: now, facing Oscar Thornton's successor, he was half-ashamed of the confusions that had sent him to the haven of a Buddhist shrine.

"The Prince tried hard to set me right," he said. "If *you'd* been a little less closemouthed, we could be running our first test now."

Chan's face lighted with the quick, warm smile John remembered from boyhood. Once again, the resemblance to his father was uncanny.

"I hoped—and so did Indra—that you'd never question my methods. After all, you accepted the presence of Chinese coolies in the ward."

"Your patients had no bearing on our experiment. Finding Shanghai labels on your culture media was something else again. Incidentally, just how did you obtain those Chlorella vials?"

"They came direct from the Peoples' Institute of Agronomy. The bureau headed by Dr. T. K. Yu."

"Has he guessed why you asked for them?"

"Only that I'm running check series on algae."

"Did he see your convertor on his last visit?"

"No, John. At that time, it didn't even exist."

"Would you say our secret's airtight, as of now?"

"Completely. I saw to it, before I asked you here."

"Just what does that statement mean?"

"From the start, I foresaw the need of workable security methods, if you gave your all to my experiment. As an American, you'd be bound to exact that condition."

"You were an American yourself, not too long ago."

"Legally I still am," said Chan. "I happen to think as an Asian. Our food-bomb concept—to borrow your technician's term—is a staggering one. Are you sure you've grasped it?"

"I'm sure of this much. It should be packed in cotton wool —and handled with care, like all explosives."

99

"That sounds like a quotation from Ngo Singh."

"The Prince is a philosopher, as well as a statesman," John said. "Yesterday, he repeated his conviction that our discovery—if it fulfills its purpose—could change the world's face."

"What can it do for America? A country that stores its rotting grain by the ton—and pays its farmers *not* to farm?"

"We're bound to need help eventually. The East doesn't have a patent on population explosions."

"Would you share it meanwhile?"

"Of course, once the process was perfected."

"Can you be sure Congress would be that liberal if a country like China needed help? Or one of America's half-friends, like India?"

"Fortunately for our peace of mind, Chan, we'd have no part in such policy."

"So your function would end, once you'd delivered a workable technique to Washington. Suppose you were ruler of this satrapy? Wouldn't you search your soul a bit deeper?"

"And send unlimited dried algae into Yunnan, as you've been sending rice?"

"My question was naïve. Of course *you* could never permit that indiscretion. I should have realized as much from the start."

John leaned forward intently. Chan's smile could not have been more disarming, but he could not help feeling there was still a missing point of contact.

"Let's get one thing clear. This discovery isn't ours to bestow."

Chan spread his hands in a gesture of dismissal. "You reached Muong Toa just in time, John. I told Indra as much this morning. Only yesterday, I had dreams of using this valley as a guinea pig. Proving I was a good shepherd, in a way my father never could."

"You've already given such proof."

"How do you mean?"

"I saw your notes on the diet test yesterday. They were in a file one of your technicians gave me. I couldn't resist reading them."

"Those were small-scale tests, John. So small, I was ashamed to mention them."

"You had three hundred volunteers in each village. The rice diet produced twenty-one cases of beriberi—and other effects of vitamin-lack. Those who ate dried algae stayed well, and their work-charts showed a marked rise in output. I'd call such figures fairly conclusive."

"I think now I should have waited—until the mutation could be harvested in quantity. This summer, I'd like to run a much larger test—using different ethnic groups, at factory as well as farming level."

"Do you see now that such procedure would be impossible?"

"Would it be feasible in the States?"

The question was a challenge, and John knew it was justified. "We're both aware of the difficulties," he said patiently. "Test centers might be set up in South America, or the Philippines."

"Politics aside, you must admit China would be an ideal proving ground."

"With India a close second."

"But you'd give our discovery to neither country, if the choice were yours?"

"I won't have to make that choice. Nor will you."

"Answer the question, John."

Cornered at last, the microbiologist forced himself to speak firmly.

"Not with their present leaders."

"Not even if the gift would outlaw starvation, for all time? The freedom-from-hunger groups in America would vote you down. I'm even told the President is considering a distribution of surplus grain in China, to save lives."

"Surplus grain is one matter, Chan. Food Unlimited is quite another. Let's remember that man doesn't live by bread alone."

"What does that homily signify?"

"I'm telling you that man's salvation must be earned. It can't be spelled out by brute force in Peiping. Nor can it be won by India's withdrawal from the battle."

The younger Thornton's smile was gently reproving now. His last gesture of dismissal was a weary one—the sorrow of a man of goodwill for all human failing.

"Is that another quotation from our philosopher-prince?"

"The thoughts are my own, Chan. They may not be original, but they're cogent. When this mutation is pinned down —if it can be pinned—I insist on taking our formula to Washington. I'm thanking God I can leave its use thereafter to higher authority. In the meantime, no one's to hear a word of it. If that makes me an ugly American, I can't help myself."

"It makes you a prudent American, John. I've already agreed to your terms. You'll find my prudence will match your own. Now can we get on with the job?"

There was an air of waiting in the laboratory that struck John between the eyes. That morning, the native technicians had deserted their tasks to stare at Dudley Porter, who was in the act of checking the last connection of the new burner complex. John saw that Chan had responded to the challenge: when he entered the inner alcove, his shoulders were squared like a man facing battle.

Indra sat at her usual place at the worktable, with her notebook open. Dud was on hands and knees among the tentacles of the convertor. The faded jumper he was wearing suggested an auto mechanic rather than a man of science. His eyes were sparkling behind their horn-rims.

"It's time you turned up, John," he said. "In two more minutes, we'll be cooking with gas."

The microbiologist gave the apparatus a quick survey. His assistant had labored hard in his absence. At three-foot intervals, he had attached clusters of small ducts to each of the major culture tubes, using a plastic sealer to make the joints airtight. The ducts, in turn, led to the intake of the new jet burner, which Dud had set up in the courtyard as part of Chan's own furnace. Attached to the burner's turbine was a set of cogwheels: when the burner was in action, they would turn the centrifuges of the convertor.

"You're sure those smaller tubes will draw, Dud?"

102

"Miss Lal and I just gave them a trial. They're sharp as leeches."

"Is the furnace fired?"

"Ready and waiting," said Dud. "Feed the monster, and we're in business."

John met each pair of eyes in turn. "I take it we all have the picture," he said quietly. "First, we draw the methane gas into the furnace—as fast as it forms, we hope. By burning it, we'll prevent an explosion in the convertor; we also step up our supply of carbon dioxide—enough, we hope, to harvest a bumper crop of algae. The energy created will also drive the centrifuges, separating culture medium from full-grown cells. Finally, we'll have extra heat to dry the harvest." He turned to Chan, who had leaned against the worktable with folded arms, his lips set in a taut smile. "Did I exaggerate, when I said my man Friday was a genius?"

"The idea was yours, John," Dud Porter protested. "All I did was fill out the pattern."

"It's a fine job, Dud. If it blows up in our faces, I'll take the blame. Let's see how well it moves."

Indra had left her post to direct the two technicians who waited with the first batch of culture medium—a carefully measured amount of the Chlorella mutation on which their hopes rested. At her order, they put the heavy flask in John's hands. Balancing it on the edge of the vat that held the nutrient for the test run, he noted that the culture was quiescent.

"We'll go slow at first," he said. "Even with Dud's help, this could be a ticklish business." He shook half the culture into the vat—and stood aside, until Indra had stirred it thoroughly into the mixture. Dud had started the main pump. When he dropped the intake hose into the vat, the now-activated medium siphoned into the maw of the convertor, then pulsed into its radiating arms. In another moment, the tubes, fed by the monster's heartbeat, were dancing with a life of their own.

The technicians had wheeled the empty culture vat aside and brought another into place. John shook his head as Dud

103

held up the intake hose. Setting the mutation flask on a shelf, he joined his assistant among the plastic coils.

"We'll watch how fast this develops," he said. "Is the pump still at half-speed?"

"Half-speed it is, Boss."

"You'd better open the water intake. We'll want to keep the contents of those tubes diluted."

When Dud had moved to the valve, John kept his place among the now fast-writhing coils. Dud, with his trained eye, would maintain an even flow, balancing water against culture medium. It was John's task to watch for the first sign of danger in the tubes. Already sunlight was beginning to glow through the wafer-thin plastic, showing that the fluid charge had begun its lethal production of methane.

"Cut in the jet," he ordered. "You were right when you called our *bat jhow yee* a gasser."

"Easy does it, Boss. We'll relieve that gut-ache pronto."

In the courtyard, the jet burner went into action with a whining roar that suggested a plane's takeoff. The relief had not come too soon: section after section of the tubing had begun to bulge alarmingly, taking on a baleful iridescence as it distended to the bursting point with methane from fast-decomposing cells. Then, as the clusters of taping tubes performed their function, the dead-white tentacles resumed their normal contours. In the court, the stepped-up whine of the burner relayed the news that the circuit was completed. Thanks to Dud's wizardry, the octopus had cast off its first major illness without missing a heartbeat.

At the water valve, Dud lifted two fingers in a victory sign.

"It's impossible—but it's happening."

"Now you know how I felt, the day I had to slash the tubing."

"I'll bet you set a record."

So far, not all the plastic exposure had filled; but John noted with satisfaction that some of the fluid culture had already dropped into the settling tank, a sure sign that it was heavy with fully grown cells. Here and there, he saw a bubble of methane that had escaped the tapping tubes. On the

104

whole, the fluid seemed clean as the finale of a normal run.

When the first settling tank was filled, he shifted the hose to another. A technician came forward promptly, to draw off the supernatant fluid and transfer the solid cells to the centrifuge. The whole room shook when the arms began to turn at top speed, but John could ignore this stage of the run. Before Indra could add the balance of the mutation medium to the new culture vat, he was back among the coils, watching for the next sign of distention.

As he had feared, the movement of the culture, despite the best efforts of the pump, had begun to slow to some degree. The threat of an explosion had been lost in the devouring flame of the jet burner, but it was evident that some of the cells within those swollen tubes were degenerating too rapidly to reach full growth. The harvesting, of course, would continue. The exciting tempo of that first yield had already been lost.

"What's happening, John? Is there a kickback?"

It was Chan who had spoken, in a voice that was not quite his own. John realized it was the first word his friend had uttered.

"We'll have our answer when this batch is dried. Everything depends on its weight—and its ratio to the original fluid volume."

"You know there's been a slowdown. The yield's bound to be lower than we hoped."

John threw a quick glance across the squat body of the convertor. It was unlike Chan to give way to frustration so openly. Before he could answer, Dud spoke up, above the hard beat of the centrifuges.

"This run is just for size, Dr. Thornton. Try to keep loose."

"What does *keep loose* mean?"

"Like a batter who won't be spooked when a pitcher throws beanballs."

Chan stared for a moment at John's assistant, as though the man had spoken gibberish. Then he began to stride up and down the alcove, with his back turned to his co-workers. When John glanced toward Indra, he saw that a frown had creased her forehead. Stepping from his observation post, he addressed her in a whisper.

"Can't you calm Chan down? This isn't a matter of life or death."

"It is to him, John."

When the trays had emerged from the dryer, Chan was still pacing restlessly in the same self-imposed exile from the workroom. Busy with a score of details, John had found no time to soothe that crisis of nerves. Now, moving to check the contents of the settling tank, he knew his friend was peering over his shoulder. He needed only a glance to realize the convertor was now producing at a rate far short of its optimum level.

"Shouldn't we step up the charge?" Chan's question was mild enough: John could sense the tension behind it.

"Let's get the figures on this first run," he said easily. "At least we've proved our jet burner can handle a by-product like methane. Maybe that's achievement enough for one morning."

"I'll weigh the harvest, if you like."

"Do, please. I'll give you readings from the slide rule."

One of the technicians had just brought the first tray to the scale, heaped with its familiar mound of powder. Chan shouldered him aside and bent above the weights. The ritual of weighing, like John's automatic tabulation from the slide rule, was a reflex action to cover a numbing disappointment. Both doctors had already realized that the heaps of greenish powder, though they seemed more bountiful than previous yields, showed no real improvement in the process.

"What went sour, John?"

"Apparently the cells aren't getting enough carbon dioxide. That's why so many of them decompose."

"All we've done, then, is produce methane—and burn it."

"You could put it that way." John had spoken gently, aware that Chan's voice (and his temper) was rising with each word.

"Can *you* make a better diagnosis?"

The microbiologist ignored the sarcasm. "That jet engine

outside is eating up methane—and loving it. Right now, it's giving off more than enough $CO_2$ for unlimited photosynthesis. It just isn't reaching the individual cells fast enough, coming as it does through the main body of the convertor."

"We had that same headache in Frisco," said Dud. "Remember *our* first runs, John? When the culture turned to mush and refused to budge?"

"It's doing the same thing now," said Chan, and his voice was just under a shout. "Your new gadgets have failed." He stalked toward the door of the lab. "I'm going to have a smoke—in fresh air. Let me know if you get another brainstorm." The door slammed behind him resoundingly enough to shake every vial on the worktable. No one spoke until the sound had died.

"Does he always bug this easy?" Dud asked.

"Not always," John answered. "Remember, he's been fighting algae a long time."

"So have we, Boss. So has Miss Lal. *She's* calm and collected."

"Should I bring him back, Indra?"

The girl shook her head. "Give him five minutes, John. He'll tell you he's sorry."

"The lady's right, I hope," said Dud. "Meanwhile, let's try to marry $CO_2$ with this hopped-up Chlorella—and make sure it's a happy wedding."

John had been circling the convertor, studying the still-quivering tentacles, as the last of the test run inched down their length. Dud's flippancy had rung a bell in his mind. So far, he could hear no more than the echo.

"We can't bring the cells any closer to the carbon dioxide. Is there some way to bring it to them?"

"You name it, Boss," said Dud. "I'll work it out."

"Any suggestions, Indra?"

"Perhaps a few pins would help."

"*Pins?*"

"Sorry. I was thinking aloud. Dr. Porter wouldn't need actual pins. We've surgical needles in the stock room."

"Are you suggesting we puncture the convertor?"

"I was remembering something from freshman physics. I

107

believe it's called the tube-within-a-tube principle." Indra had joined John in the court; now she touched one of the bloated tentacles with her toe. "Suppose you took lengths of *small* tubing, filled them with perforations, and ran them through each of these larger tubes. You could pump $CO_2$ direct to the culture medium—not just to the convertor, as we're doing now."

Dud bounded from the alcove and shook Indra's hand. "I should have fielded that one on my own," he said. "With carbon dioxide bubbling in its midst, every cell in the mixture will be free to grow."

"Then you think it will work?"

"It's got to, this time." Dud cut the main switch of the convertor. "Of course, it means taking the whole complex apart and starting over, but that's why lab men were born."

"How long will you need?" John asked.

"Two hours, maybe three. That is, if I can recruit a few pinprickers."

"I'll enlist, for one," said John. "I'm sure Miss Lal is a good needlewoman."

"If you don't mind," said the girl, "we'll excuse you for a moment. It's time you talked to Chan."

The microbiologist found his friend on the bottom step of the vestibule. His shoulder was propped against the doorjamb, and an unlighted cigarette had crumbled to shreds in his nervous fingers.

"You might have let me come to you," he said. "I'm almost ready to apologize. I've been under a strain lately—for more than one reason."

Their eyes met in an unhappy duel, but the thought that Chan had all but voiced remained unspoken. *You've guessed about Indra,* John told him silently. *You guessed years ago: now I've come back, you're sure. When we were boys together, you'd never give up your possessions. You won't surrender her lightly, even though you've never loved her.*

"You'll feel better in harness," he said at last. "Shall we get to work again?"

"Why go back? I've unleashed a force that can't be harnessed. A thing that destroys faster than it builds."

108

"The world won't stop if we fail, Chan."

"If we'd succeeded, we might have *saved* the world."

"I haven't abandoned hope. Indra and Dud are willing to go on. Why aren't you?"

"After today's fiasco?"

"This isn't the first experiment to kick back in the early stages."

"I've worked for years with algae—and gotten nowhere."

"So did Ehrlich with 606. And Fleming, before he discovered penicillin."

"Those were microbe-killers, John. Food Unlimited would have given life."

"Perhaps we can still make the gift. Why not come back and find out? I want your advice on a new approach Indra suggested."

Chan listened in brooding silence while John described the tube-within-a-tube device.

"Does Dr. Porter think it's practical?"

"He's sure of it."

"How do you know the degenerative process won't continue?"

"It could still happen, of course. Our approach is tentative, but it's an answer to your diagnosis. It's just possible we can start nature's cycle moving naturally again."

"Assuming the carbon dioxide hits each cell before it's too late."

"Dud says it's physically feasible. Once the method's perfected, it could increase our yield a hundredfold."

Chan's head lifted at last. When his face broke into its familiar grin, John saw his black mood had vanished.

"Thanks for the verbal hypo," he said. "You'll have no cause to complain of me again." He took the key from his ring, unlocked the padlock, and marched into the laboratory.

John stood for a moment more in the half-open portal, smoking a well-earned cigarette while he weighed the reasons for that sudden lift in spirits. Then hearing the whine of the jet burner (as Dud Porter cautiously tested the first of his new couplings), he followed Chan into the alcove that had become their private world.

The work of reassembling the convertor was arduous. In the end, Dud found that over three hours were needed to thread the small, perforated tubes inside the multiple arms of the octopus. Special ingenuity was needed to extend the life-giving carbon dioxide to the last solar segment in the court-yard, and extra sealings were required at each joint to prevent the gas from escaping before it could perform its vital function. It was midafternoon before John felt ready to risk another test run. Even then, despite their rigorous precautions, he watched it with fingers crossed, lest the roaring furnace touch off a detonation in some pocket Dud had overlooked.

On the whole, the results were heartening. With $CO_2$ bubbling into the culture through a thousand tiny openings, there was no visible backup in the major tentacles. Inevitably some sluggishness remained, particularly in those sections farthest from the pump, where the formation of methane continued with the same maddening persistence. But there was no mistaking the increased yield, when the trays of dried algae were brought to the scales.

Dud Porter's face was a mask of exhaustion after the last run, but his voice boomed with good spirits.

"We've still bugs to spare," he said. "I expected that. The big problem, as of now, is to maintain an even pressure head in the delivery tube: to be really efficient, we must force the gas to the limit. Our friend the octopus is a lot healthier than she was this morning, but she still has a few gouty toes, so to speak. That's another ailment we'll try to cure tomorrow."

Chan, who had worked through the day without a whisper of doubt, looked up from his notes.

"Shouldn't there be some correlation between your pressure head and the number of perforations in the smaller tubes?"

"Right, Dr. Thornton. The mathematics of that one will take me awhile to figure."

"At least we know the process is feasible. You've demonstrated that much brilliantly."

John's assistant flushed with pleasure. To hide his reaction, he moved to the outer court to check the gauge on the oven.

"Even on this trial heat, we've exceeded expectations," he said. "Give me a few days with a slide rule, and I'll have this old girl pumping through hoops. One thing we must keep in mind: the faster the run, the less methane we'll produce. In the long view, that means less $CO_2$ from the jet burner. Eventually, we'll hit on the ideal speed. That's our present target."

Hours of work remained before the convertor could be readied for the next day's trials. With the help of the others, Dud rechecked each inch of small tubing, to make sure his perforation count was accurate. It was well past the dinner hour before they could charge the convertor from a standby vat. Ovens and pump were both cut to half-speed to provide the basis for the first morning run. When he had added the last measure of culture medium and noted the final valve pressures, John found it was close to midnight.

Chan had left at nine to make his hospital rounds with Dr. Vong, promising to nap on his office couch before returning. Indra had been ordered to her bed in the nurses' home at eleven. As for John's assistant, he had rested for two after-dinner hours on a shakedown bunk. When he returned to his work-stool at the stroke of twelve, he seemed alert as a freshman at a football rally.

"You've no right to look so refreshed, Dud."

"Napoleon took catnaps at every battle. Why can't I? It's your turn now."

John pushed his notes across the table and tried to rub weariness from his eyelids.

"Perhaps I should wait for Chan."

"He promised to sleep until four. Don't let me see your face until nine tomorrow. We'll want your brain in high gear for the new countdown."

"I wouldn't look forward to anything spectacular."

The technician removed his horn-rims, and blinked at John above the cones of the work-lights. "I asked you once to call it a night. Our opinions will keep."

"*Yours* won't, Dud. I want it now."

"We aren't home free, of course. New headaches are sure to develop tomorrow. But a first-year science major could see the runaway's under control."

"Control is one thing. Taming's quite another. Even with

the increased harvest, we're still wrestling with an outlaw."

"This baby's no longer outside the law, John. For more than three months, it's bred true. It's part of the vegetable kingdom now, just like those new elements atomic fission created. *Our* job it to make it turn respectable. So respectable, it'll do a useful job, like any citizen."

"Some mavericks can never be tamed, Dud."

"This one will answer the bit eventually, Boss, take my word. I'll add a second hunch, while I'm about it. Once our control is absolute, the sky's the limit."

"Shall I pass on that judgment to Chan?"

"By all means. Now he's settled down, he'll do his job."

"We can count on that, I'm sure."

"I'll even take back the harsh words I used this morning, when he pulled rank on us. With the investment he has here, I'd probably have done the same."

"From a human Univac like yourself," said John, "that's a handsome concession."

"This job will *need* a Univac—until we've written our final equation. For the last time, will you hit the sack?"

John crossed the compound in time to meet Chan on the clinic porch.

"Dud tells me you promised to sleep until four," he said accusingly.

"I'll catch a nap, after I've looked over his shoulder."

"All quiet in the wards?"

"Vong can handle the hospital tonight." Chan glanced toward the guest bungalow, where a pencil of light showed behind the shutters. "If I were you, I'd head straight for my own room. Your Mr. Wilde might intercept you."

"When did Lex get in?"

"Just before sunset, by special charter. Didn't you hear the plane motor?"

John shook his head—and stifled a prodigious yawn. "It seems I've blanked out on externals since noon. To be honest, I'd forgotten Lex Wilde existed."

"You'll find he's still a nuisance," said Chan. "I've just warned him this part of the compound's out of bounds."

"Let's hope I'll be as strong-minded."

Even in the uncertain gleam of the porch light, John was aware of the abrupt lift of Chan's brows.

"Perhaps I ought to deport him after all."

"He's less dangerous here than outside. At least we can control his snooping, even if we can't edit his prose."

"I can do the next best thing," said Chan. "He'll send out no more copy on the shortwave, until it's cleared with me."

"Do you think that's wise?"

"Wilde has guessed too much now, John. Do you want this story to break prematurely, when the result's in the balance?"

Chan moved on without waiting for an answer, pausing on the laboratory stoop to open and close the padlocks. Across the lawn, Lex Wilde's typewriter began to chatter busily. For an instant, John found his rebel footsteps were leading him toward the guesthouse, if only to soften the impact of Chan's harsh ruling. Then, admitting the soundness of his friend's advice, he turned toward his own quarters.

Eight hours later, the aroma of coffee reached him in what had seemed a bottomless pit of slumber.

For a little longer, a compulsive need for withdrawal forced him to cling to sleep like a drug. Then, without transition, he found he was sitting upright in the misty ambush of his mosquito netting. Lex Wilde stood at his bedside, in the act of pouring from a copper pot.

"Don't say I spoiled your rest." The journalist parted the netting to give John a cup. "I waited for you to waken naturally."

"Does Chan know you're here?"

"Why should he? Is the new king of Muong Toa your warden?"

"Last midnight, he suggested I give you a wide berth. Unfortunately I was too tired to lock my door."

"Aren't you going to ask me for my news?"

"Did you go to Bangkok as you planned?"

"My stay there was brief," said Wilde. "There were too many envious reporters clamoring for tips at the Deux

113

Mondes. In the circumstances, it seemed logical to charter a pilot and return at once."

"You could have saved yourself a trip, Lex. It's highly unlikely we'll have a story for you by Friday."

"What's Friday to do with it?"

"It was your deadline, I believe. Aren't you covering the President's speech in Paris?"

"The NATO meeting's been called off until June, so I can wait out Operation Chlorella on the spot. My editor ordered me to sit tight until you open up."

Remembering Chan's determination to close the shortwave, John continued to study the cup between his palms.

"You simply won't believe you're only marking time here?"

"Not with Dud Porter knee-deep in new equipment across the way. I could ask some pointed questions about that jet burner you're using, but I'll remember our bargain."

"Who told you we're using a jet burner?"

"After all, John, it makes its own music."

The microbiologist threw the netting aside. "If you'll excuse me, Lex, I'll head for the shower."

"Not until you hear all my news—and interpret it. My plane was buzzed on the way in."

"Over Laos?"

"While we were following the Mekong Valley. My charter was from Thailand, and plainly marked. Isn't that rather strange behavior during a *de facto* truce?"

"Come off it, Lex. Hanoi has been using the Laotian Corridor for years—to filter its killers into South Vietnam. You were lucky to find an air lane."

"The plane that buzzed me was Russian-made—an Ilyushin 14."

"Russian airlifts have been helping the Pathet Lao for some time. It's hardly news that you tangled with an Ilyushin in the Corridor."

"You're taking this a damn sight more calmly than I did," said the journalist. "That pilot made two runs at our wingtips. For a while, I was sure he'd open fire."

"Considering your profession, Lex, you must have been shot at before."

114

"I'm sure that fellow had word I was heading back here. Obviously, it was a not too subtle warning to clear out."

"Are you taking the hint?"

"No, damn it. I sent my charter back at sunrise. I'm going to stay in Muong Toa until you close up shop. Meanwhile, I want just one honest answer. Haven't you had the feeling things are closing in here?"

"By no means."

"In other words, you think Peiping intends to spare this particular rice bowl, so long as it continues to feed Yunnan Province?"

"Muong Toa always has sent food to Yunnan."

"What if Thornton builds another rice bowl in that lab—big enough to feed the world? His friends in China will expect to get the first helping."

John felt his temper rise, even as common sense warned him the query was only an educated guess. Fixing Wilde with an icy glare, he rose from his cot and reached for a bathrobe.

"Speaking of the lab, I'm due there now."

"My needling was premature," said Wilde. "I don't expect an answer. But I'm asking why your alleged friend insists on censoring my dispatches. Last night, he threatened to close the shortwave if I file columns on anything stronger than the local peach harvest."

"I'd say that was his right."

"There are nasty names for such censorship, John. Fascism's one of the milder ones."

"There's no need to call Chan names, just because he gives the orders here. If you must know, I'm glad to see you muzzled."

"Back him to the end, then. In your place, I'd admit friendship has limits."

In the shower, John felt his mind veer toward a familiar gambit as the impact of Wilde's acute guesses sank home. The spasm of doubting was brief: this morning, with a new test run impending, it was easy to close his mind to externals. The work awaiting him across the compound was all the burden he could bear.

# 5.

THREE days—and a score of test runs—later, John was forced to the conviction that he must make haste slowly if the experiment was to break new ground.

The admission was sobering. From the start, sparked by Chan's driving need for results, they had been fighting a process that insisted on setting its own timetable. Instinct told him the final answer would be simple: the steps to the solution could be endless. Until the information necessary to that solution had been gleaned, they would continue to move in circles. John could understand why the skin on Chan's cheekbones seemed more drawn, and why the shadows beneath Indra's eyes grew deeper. At times, even Dud Porter seemed to stagger while he checked the convertor for yet another trial.

Mathematics, John knew, is the parent science of all research. In this battle to harness the force of the mutation, it might be their nemesis or their savior, but their cause was hopeless until they admitted its primacy. It was impossible to solve their problem as a whole, merely by adjusting the *bat jhow yee* to the diverse factors involved.

First was the growth-rate of the mutation itself, a phenomenon to which Dud could only assign the symbol of infinity, in itself an admission of defeat. This, of course, was their basic stumbling block: it had been impossible, so far, to measure a performance that literally exploded when supplied with all its needs. Again and again, Dud had sought to pin down the pattern with hypothetical numbers: the actual growth-figure remained an unknown, thanks to the limitless power Chan's X ray had created.

Not that Chan's feat was unique: the mutation, John realized, was only another natural force gone berserk. The root that split the city sidewalk, the tendril that choked a stately

116

dwelling, the jungle that reduced a Mayan pyramid to powder—these, too, were proofs of nature's blind might, and both poet and scientist could accept them. In the case of the mutation, it had been wishful thinking to hope that its potential could be tamed even before it could be measured.

Factor after factor had been established before it was worked into one of the tentative equations Dud Porter had set down and discarded: ideal hydrogen-ion concentration; the best temperature before and during the run; light-energy balance; the quantity of $CO_2$ best suited for cell division; the exact amount of methane needed for combustion in the jet burner, to produce that carbon dioxide. Hundreds of feeder tubes were employed before Dud was satisfied with the size and the placing of each tiny puncture. From the first run, he had seen that too many perforations diminished the pressure head of the gas, cutting the supply in the more remote areas of solar exposure.

Perhaps the worst problem was the warring presence of both methane and carbon dioxide in the cycle. Too generous an infusion of the latter gas slowed the degeneration of the cells, but the resulting lack of methane (and its dilution by excess $CO_2$) brought a drop in the efficiency of the jet burner and the centrifuges. Too rapid degeneration, of course, cut into the final harvest-yield. Once again, the need was balance. Until that ideal was discovered, Dud Porter would hang on the horns of a mathematical dilemma.

Late on the afternoon of the third day (when clouds had blotted sunlight from the Enchanted Valley), John ordered a halt until morning. The native technicians could use the time to good advantage, since the convertor was in need of cleaning before the next major run. The team, at his express command, was to forget the project entirely. To insure compliance, he had asked Indra to plan a special dinner, with Lex Wilde as an invited guest. The journalist's presence, he reminded the others, would make discussion of their work verboten. It was even agreed that the mere mention of science, in any form, would exact a dollar fine from the offender.

The meal, starting with cocktails on the veranda, and ending with a magnificent Canton duck, had roused echoes of less

117

troubled days. Indra, in a green silk sari, with her dark hair piled high and caught in a jade tiara, had been an ideal chatelaine. Presiding at the table's head (and looking his best in a white dinner coat) Chan Thornton had been the epitome of the urbane host. Now, as the houseboys cleared the table and brought in coffee and liqueurs, he addressed Lex Wilde with the same easy camaraderie.

"May we have a preview of your next column, since we're all avid readers? I'll withdraw my request, if it's conducive to ulcers."

"On the contrary, Doctor," said Wilde. "*This* is a column I'm positive you won't censor."

"What I can't understand is how you turn out eight hundred words every other day—without a soupçon of news."

"It's part of my business to find news in odd corners. Tomorrow's column will use this dinner party as its springboard."

"Surely the table talk of four research workers isn't newsworthy."

"Don't think I'm asking how your day went, Dr. Thornton. I'm too well schooled to repeat that blunder. What really interests me is the fact the four of you have joined forces, that you can dine together at day's end and talk as friends. Doesn't that raise a hope—however faint—that the human race will someday do likewise?"

"How soon, Mr. Wilde?" Chan asked. "After some million years of upright existence, the human animal seems just as suspicious of his neighbor. How can he be trained to follow the example of such paragons as ourselves?"

Watching the journalist closely, John realized that he was accepting Chan's baiting for a purpose of his own. On the surface, his manner seemed completely ingenuous.

"I'll admit it's a dream, Dr. Thornton. It still seems worth voicing."

"How would you extend your area of friendship?"

"By a true meeting of minds. Tonight we've a brotherhood of science in this remote corner of southeast Asia. Why not a brotherhood of man tomorrow—at the conference table?"

118

"Based on what political system—the theory of democracy?"

"Can you think of a better one?"

Dud Porter reached for the brandy and poured his second glass. "Wasn't it Bernard Shaw who said that democracy was like Christianity? Both of them hopeful charts for human conduct, even though neither has been tried?"

"Such cynicism is unworthy of your years," said Indra.

"We in America pose as examples of equality, Miss Lal. Yet we give our wool-hats the vote—and refuse it to Negro professors. Perhaps you can dig the difference. It's beyond my mousetrap mind."

Wilde chuckled at the exchange. "No method of government is perfect," he said. "Democracy may seem more vulnerable than most: as a realist, I must admit its occasional perversions. I still maintain it's the last, best hope of man. Does Dr. Merchant agree?"

The journalist, John realized, had launched his round robin well, snatching the conversational ball from Chan with a dexterity few debaters could equal. Unwilling to enter the game, he found himself taking Wilde's dare.

"Dud thinks democracy's never been tried," he said. "He could be right. I still agree with Lex that our fumble in that direction has been fruitful. After all, it's less than four hundred years since the first white settlement in the United States. China has a culture that goes back to the roots of history. Simple logic would suggest a country's wisdom grows with its age—but it's obvious the Western world still retains its capacity for growth, because it has true freedom of choice. Now that China's surrendered to gangster rule, it's slipping into barbarism. Recent events suggest it could go over the edge at any time."

"What are you trying to prove?"

"Let me answer for him," said Wilde. (He was writing as he talked: John knew he was setting down his own remarks verbatim.) "Imagine a really free election, in any captive area of the globe—from East Germany to Yunnan Province. If the people could speak their mind, they'd choose freedom.

If world government could assure that freedom, they'd select it above all others."

"You're a busy traveler, Mr. Wilde," said Chan. "You've covered most of the revolutions and counterrevolutions of our time. Do you honestly believe the average man could value freedom properly if it were thrust upon him tomorrow—much less use it?"

"Speak for yourself, Dr. Thornton," said the journalist. "It's a matter of record that your father's rule has done wonders in Muong Toa. From what I've seen, you've been a forthright successor. Isn't it true your people can go just so far—until they're entrusted with the management of their own affairs?"

"If the Valley were granted your brand of freedom, we'd have chaos here tomorrow. Basically, my people are still an unsolved problem in social evolution. It needs time and patience, like any enigma of science."

Lex turned to Dud Porter. "The comparison's an apt one," he said. "Will you accept it?"

"First, I'm fining Dr. Thornton a dollar," said Dud. "He just used a naughty word—*science*."

Chan laughed at the thrust. John's ear (tuned to every nuance of his friend's moods) knew the laughter was genuine. He was enjoying this game of wits with the journalist.

"I'll accept the rebuke and the fine," Chan said. "I can see Dr. Porter believes in a separation of powers, like all sensible men."

"Your world is the valley," said Dud. "Your job is to keep peace here—if possible. *My* command post is the lab: it's always kept me busy. The heavy thinkers can handle what goes on outside."

"Then you're willing to conform, if you're left alone?" Wilde asked.

"I'm content to be a good workman, and nothing more," said Dud. "A man's bound to be corrupted when he leaves his last, whether he's a cobbler or a biochemist."

"Did you say *corrupted*, Dr. Porter?" Indra asked.

"Influenced, then, if you'll pardon my semantics. Emotions always color judgment."

120

"Can't you risk being human?"

"Not in working hours."

Wilde had been making busy pothooks in his notebook. At Dud's pronouncement, he put down his pencil. The mass interview, John perceived, was getting out of hand.

"Suppose you open your lab door some fine morning and find yourself facing another Hitler?"

Dud shrugged. "It's the reverse of the coin. I'll take that risk as well."

"Would *you*, John?"

"I've followed Dud's program myself, so far," John said. "He's right, to a point. Pure science must be a world apart, if the scientist is to give his best. The minute a man begins thinking of his work in personal terms, or wondering how the world will use it, he ceases to do his job." He took a dollar from his pocket and tossed it to Dud.

"And you, Dr. Thornton?" the journalist asked.

"I'd give a great deal to make my own dedication as complete," said Chan. "John knows that's no idle boast. So, I hope, does Indra. As it happens, a few thousand half-savage people look to me for leadership. Therefore, I've no choice but to lead."

"Do you accept the dictator principle?"

"Call me a benevolent monarch without a crown," said Chan. "It has a nicer sound." He looked round the table. "What this discussion has omitted so far, I'm afraid, is the obligation of intelligence. The American constitution insists all men are created equal—a noble concept indeed. It's still a hard fact that most worldly activity proves the opposite. If a man's born with a brain, he must guide those who aren't so fortunate."

"So you think of most men as sheep, Dr. Thornton?" Wilde asked.

"I didn't quite say that. I'm merely reminding you that intelligence is a rarer commodity than the romantics will admit. When it exists, it must seek its own level."

"Then you'd endorse the biblical passage that tells us 'many are called, but few are chosen'?"

"I see nothing in human experience to refute it."

"Have you thought that Christ might revise that passage if he were living today?" John asked.

The journalist made a busy note. "Meaning that many are called—and they must choose the few?"

"I'll accept the revision, Lex. At least it gives some meaning to man's progress from the cave."

Wilde grinned as his busy pencil raced on. "You'd make a good politician, John. Let's not forget those occasions when the many must remove the few."

"Isn't that the heart of our discussion? Society will always need leaders, but they must be responsible to those who are led."

"With an important reservation," said Chan. "The power to bestow leadership, or withdraw it, will always rest with the elite."

"With people like yourself?" Wilde asked.

"People like ourselves," said the younger Thornton smoothly. "Men with the training to dream beyond tomorrow. Men who can harness the world's energies to serve their dreams."

"Men of science?"

"The fact that our scientists have taken so small a part in government is one of the tragedies of our time. John will agree, I'm sure."

The microbiologist nodded his approval of his friend's dialectic. Anticipating a label Lex Wilde was eager to bestow, he had avoided it neatly.

"I'll back Chan completely in that sentiment," he said. "Scientists have always proved their own brotherhood, in the best sense. It's too bad others can't learn from their example."

"May I make that a direct quote?" Wilde asked.

"You already have, I'm sure," John said dryly. "Unfortunately our brotherhood has always tended to be rather special. It hasn't learned the language of the people—and vice versa. Since the century's turn, the gap has widened enormously. Until it's bridged, we'll continue to be called witch doctors, the sort who weave their spells in private."

"What's your remedy?"

"First, I'd build that bridge, and make it a two-way street.

Meanwhile, I'll fight for a better life with the weapons I understand."

"Including the big bang?" Lex demanded.

"War will be made obsolete, if we endure as a species."

"By a world government?"

"You've ridden that hobbyhorse to death, Lex. World government is generations in the future. It hasn't a prayer until we've stopped Communism. Not *contained* it—stopped it cold."

"Won't containment do, John? Communism's a self-defeating evil."

"It isn't enough to put up quarantine signs. Fighting it at brush-fire level, as we're doing in southeast Asia, is a beginning—like standing pat in Berlin, and refusing to panic when Moscow plays with its bombs offstage. Those are delaying actions, not solutions. To win this nonnuclear war, we must show democracy's true face. We must make it a dream that *has* been tried."

"So freedom must prove its worth to survive?"

"That's hardly a startling conclusion," John said. "It's still the best I can offer. Either our way of life's a sure antidote for the world's despair, or we go under. We'll do just that, if we don't stop preaching and start acting."

"Isn't your remedy a bit too simple?" Wilde asked.

"All good medicine is simple. Let's stop talking about brotherhood and concentrate on men. Tom Jefferson's still quotable—but it's better to put people to work, at home and abroad. No man with a job he's proud of will turn to Communism of his own free will. If we can win the war against misery, Communism will wither on the vine, in a way Marx never dreamed of. That's been proved over and over. It's the reason Iron and Bamboo Curtains exist."

"Can your country meet the bill?" Indra asked.

"We'll have to. There's no such thing as cut-rate survival."

"If memory serves," said Chan, "you covered this same ground when we were students in Cambridge. Indra supported your views, even then. Does she still?"

"Let's hear from the lady, by all means," said Wilde. "She's yet to take sides."

123

Indra put down the brandy she had been sipping. "Considering the caliber of her guests," she said with a smile, "the lady is much too diplomatic to cast her vote. I'm glad we're still a team. As Mr. Wilde remarked, it shows there's hope for us all. If you insist, I'll risk just one opinion. We all need our sleep."

She rose from the table, bringing the men to their feet. John found himself persisting a moment more.

"Women are supposed to possess intuitions we can't share," he said. "We've expressed some high hopes tonight, Indra. Tell us whether they'll come true—or are we wasting our breath?"

"Men have wasted their breath since they invented speech," the girl said. "I'll quote just one of your remarks, then wish you all good-night. From here on, it's deeds that count— inside the lab and out. Shall we adjourn on that note?"

Like most seasoned research specialists, John had trained himself to sleep almost at will when an experiment was in progress. Since his first night in Muong Toa, he had fallen on his narrow cot in a state close to exhaustion—and, save for his poppied fantasy at the monastery, it had been a slumber without dreams. Tonight he found that an overstimulated mind (still geared to the cosmic arguments of the dinner table) refused to surrender to a tired body. When the dial of his watch stood at midnight, he pulled a robe over his pajamas and stepped through his tall screened window to count the stars.

The night was moonless. Obeying a second impulse, he waited for his eyes to adjust to the shadowed kampong, then moved toward the pergola that connected the director's residence with the hospital. For once, the windows of the journalist's room were dark. Chan's own quarters still glowed behind tight-drawn blinds. It was an obscure comfort to know that sleep had also eluded the new ruler of the Enchanted Valley.

John's feet had already found the flagstones of the pergola. Choosing the bench in the arch of bougainvillea, he lifted his eyes to the facade of the nurses' wing—and half-hoped that

Indra was sleeping soundly. Yet when a mothlike silhouette appeared in the compound gate, he felt no real surprise. Like himself, the woman he loved had good reason to walk and ponder alone.

When Indra took the pergola path, he stayed in his dark retreat, determined to let her pass without a word. She was wearing sandals and a terry-cloth robe: her hair was gathered in a loose braid and gleamed with moisture. It was not the first time she had swum at midnight in the pond above the rice paddies. Had he yielded to his own vagrant impulse, he might have found her there.

"Is it you, John?"

"Yes."

They had spoken in the barest whispers while she moved quickly to join him on the bench—fitting a shoulder to the curve of his arm as though it had belonged there always.

"Why did you walk out on us tonight?" he asked.

"*All* of you were giving Mr. Wilde copy. I called a halt before we revealed everything."

"That wasn't your only motive for leaving."

"Since you ask, I'm finding it hard to be in the same room with both you and Chan."

"Not when we're working, I trust."

"Personalities aren't important in a laboratory," the girl said. "At least, they shouldn't be. It's different when we face each other as people."

"I know it's been hard on you. After all, you're caught in the middle."

Indra breathed deep, then went on resolutely with her eyes on the starlit sky.

"Chan talked to me this afternoon. He knows we're in love. He says he knew, from the moment you returned."

"I was sure he would. Chan's no fool."

"He wants me to make a choice, John."

"Between us, you mean?"

"He reminded me it was Papa Oscar's wish that we marry."

"Was *that* his notion of a proposal?"

"There was no proposal. It was a statement of fact—-and nothing more."

"Did he threaten you?"

"I don't know what you mean."

"His word is law here, now his father's gone. Did he mention that?"

"Yes, in a way. Don't misunderstand him on purpose, darling. He *did* say he could understand why some men would play the tyrant in his place—"

"Will *he* resist the temptation.?"

"He was gentle, and very fair. He promised he'd never try to keep me here—now he sees how we feel."

"We're in the clear, then."

"If we wish, we can leave Muong Toa tomorrow."

"Shall we pack up and go, Indra?"

He felt the girl stir in the curve of his arm, as she lifted troubled eyes to meet his own.

"Tonight, I could almost say yes."

"I'd give a great deal to agree. Unfortunately, all of us are too deeply committed."

"To the laboratory—or to each other?"

"Let's say to both. We can't stir, with a new test to run. No one realizes that better than Chan Thornton."

"Must you *always* think as a biologist?"

"Right now, I can think of nothing else."

"Not even of us?"

"You can't run out on our job, Indra. There's no use trying."

"Chan thought you'd take that attitude. If you're willing to leave Dr. Porter here, they could finish between them."

"That's impossible, and Chan knows it. We've been a team from the start."

The girl sighed deeply. Already there was a hint of surrender in the sound.

"You're right, I suppose. This afternoon I was too exhausted to think our problem through."

John chose his next words with care. Obviously he had yet to penetrate to the core of Indra's agitation, though he was beginning to understand Chan Thornton's approach well enough.

"Think hard. Did Chan seem *that* anxious to get rid of me? Could it have been a means to an end?"

"Are you saying he made the offer deliberately?"

"At the moment, I'm accusing no one. I'm only asking for your reaction."

"He's confident the tests will prove out after a few more runs. Perhaps he *would* like to carry off the finale single-handed, with an assist from Dr. Porter. I can't believe he wants to shut you out."

"Would you accept his offer, if I agreed?"

"This afternoon it seemed the best solution."

"Does it now?"

"No, John."

"We'll go on as before, then—and hope for the best?"

"Since you insist, darling."

"You can breathe easier, now he's promised to release you. A few more days can't matter."

"A few days—or months? Suppose this experiment goes on forever?"

"Dud's sure we'll pin down the methane problem before the week's over. The whole process could fall into line after that."

"Suppose it doesn't?"

"We must go on fighting it, as long as there's the slightest hope. It doesn't matter if Chan and I are rivals on more than one level."

"I can see that now. I'm glad you didn't call me a coward for wanting a quick way out."

She moved into his arms for a long kiss—before they walked hand in hand to the door of the nurses' wing.

The meeting in the pergola, unsettling though it had been, brought a curious peace of mind as its aftermath. When John returned to his cot, he found he could sleep at last. Wakening in the early morning, hearing Dud Porter's rendition of "The St. Louis Blues" in the shower, he knew that the off-duty evening had worked its own therapy.

He found himself echoing the tune as he took a lab coat from the clothespress. Halfway through his dressing, he remembered this was his morning off—the day he had promised to guide Lex Wilde to the caves below the Gates of Hell. A trifle stunned by his compulsion to put on a working uniform without conscious thought, he changed to boots and a set of faded army suntans. The trip would be arduous even though they could cover most of it by Rover.

The journalist was waiting at the corner table in the dining room. He was deep in a stack of carbons: judging by his rapt look, it was one of his own compositions.

"Did Chan clear your column?"

"The minute I typed it last evening." Lex held up the carbons triumphantly. "Would *you* care to check on my reporting?"

"Only if you insist," John said ungraciously. "We've a fair distance to cover—if you plan to see the caves."

"I'm holding you to that tour. You'll have time for a reading while I bring your breakfast."

The column, John found, was standard Wilde: datelined from Muong Toa, it was a winnowed transcript of last night's table talk, with John as the star performer. Much was made of the fact that a team of East-West scientists could live and work in amity. In Lex's glib paraphrase, John was made to describe this as an augury for a happier future. The hope for a lessening of international tensions was allowed to stand alone. John's insistence that Western man must fight, if need be, for his principles—and his dismissal of Communism as an outmoded prison for the spirit—were omitted entirely.

Accepting eggs and coffee, he stifled an automatic protest. Thanks to the magic of electronics, he knew these words were already in print—in the syndicated space where the ersatz rhetoric of Alexander Wilde was gospel. The direct quotations were accurate. It was futile to argue that Wilde's expert elision had made John seem a credulous idealist, willing to accept shadows for reality.

"I'd call that column one of my better efforts," said the journalist. "Of course you helped no end. You were in fine form last night."

"So were you," said John dourly.

"Haven't I done you justice?"

"I've no quarrel with what you said, Lex. It's what you left out that makes the difference. Lab workers have made up

East-West teams before. It hardly means that peace is just around the corner."

"Wouldn't you be pleased if it were?"

"Of course. Just as I'd be happy if I could invent a drug to dissolve human greed."

"You'll be doing just that in Thornton's lab, if all goes well."

"Put away the needle, please. Chan was right when he wanted to deport you."

Wilde pocketed his carbons with the air of a man protecting a sacred relic.

"I'll settle for a look at those caves today," he said. "Just remember your protective coloration is wearing thin. It won't last forever."

"Why did you ask me to plan this excursion? You're neither a geologist nor a nature lover."

"Frankly, I want a closer look at those famous Gates of Hell."

"The border's off limits. I'll be your guide, but you've got to take orders."

Lex preserved an unaccustomed silence in the Land Rover, breaking it only for queries on the natural wonder they were about to inspect. Grudgingly John admitted the newsman had good reasons for visiting these caverns, hollowed before the dawn of time by the torrent that had once raged between the Gates. In that remote era, he explained, the gorge had merited its infernal label. A million years ago (if one could believe the geologists) it had even compared with that masterwork of the devil, the American Grand Canyon.

"Don't expect the caves to stand up to legend today," he warned. "They've eroded to normal dimensions long ago."

"The books say they were once the source of an underground river."

"I've read they served as a model for the 'sacred Alph' in Coleridge's poem."

"The river that wound through stately pleasure-domes to a sunless sea?"

"Use the comparison if you like. There's no doubt that Kublai Khan passed this way not too long ago."

"He lived in the thirteenth century, John."

"That's day-before-yesterday in the Valley."

The trail the microbiologist had chosen led toward the monastery, then forked sharply to follow the flanks of the northern hills. It was a hazardous path, but he preferred it to the valley road, which pointed straight to the border. Chan had refused to give Lex Wilde access to this second route.

"Can we see China *now*, John?"

"You might, if you could soar above that line of deodars on the next ridge."

"We could get a better view from the mountaintop."

"It's too far to climb today."

John braked the Rover where the rutted trail ended. Ahead, the ridges marched in gray-green majesty to merge with Butterfly Mountain. To the right, a footpath spiraled down to the valley floor, where the twin *massifs* of the Gates brooded above their jungle-choked defile. The cliff where the monastery stood (though less than a half-mile to the west) was screened by the thrust of the nearest ridge.

The journalist, unlimbering his binoculars, let out his breath in an awed whistle.

"You were right, John. This is old man Satan's handiwork. You can read his signature in brimstone."

"The Gates are leftovers from the first buckling of the earth's crust. As I told you, erosion's reduced them to a fraction of their size."

"How far is the frontier from this point?"

"A few miles, as the crow flies. There's no formal border. Most of this area is still unmapped."

"If we followed the path below us, would we stop a bullet?"

"We're not taking that risk. And put away your Leica."

"You promised me a set of negatives, John."

"Only of the caves. *They're* well off the trail to Yunnan."

"Was that jungle trace once a highroad?"

"The Great Khan left his hoofprints there. So did the Khmer kings who fought his descendants."

"Dr. Thornton's tires have also made their mark—if that isn't an anticlimax."

130

"For the last time, this is a journey to the past. Will you follow me?"

Forced to lead the way, John descended the first slope warily. On the hillside, the air had been cool enough: once the dank jungle enclosed them, the heat pounced remorselessly. Years ago, he recalled, the monks had used the nearer caves as underground gardens, where they had cultivated a species of mushroom prized in the Valley. Even in his youth, the practice had been abandoned, but there was still a faint trail to the mouth of the first cavern, a yawning aperture huge as a cathedral door and masked by clinging vines.

"I thought you told me these caves were deserted, John."

"Except for a ghost or two. Some of them were used as tombs a long time ago."

"This is a strange graveyard—with a sentinel on guard. Or could it be a sniper?"

John's glance shifted in response to the columnist's gesture. There was no mistaking the purpose of the figure on the ledge above them. While the two visitors continued to look skyward, another armed man came into view, to stand beside the first.

"Who goes there?"

The second guard had barked the question, in French patois. John fumbled for a handkerchief, which he raised above his head.

"We are from Dr. Thornton's kampong, and we come in peace."

"I'd advise you to go no farther, Dr. Merchant."

The words were spoken from a thornbush beside the trail. Forcing himself to move casually, John turned to face the newest challenger—a wiry young man who had already stepped across the trail, his hand resting lightly on the stock of an American rifle.

"I was planning to show Dr. Thornton's guest the caves. Why is it forbidden?"

*Mille pardons,* Doctor. This land belongs to the monastery. No visitors are permitted, by order of the abbot."

"Does the abbot enforce his rules with firearms?"

"In these times, we must abandon old customs. The caves

of the Gateway are burial grounds for the Meo. They cannot be violated by strangers."

John turned to the journalist, who, for once, seemed unready to take a single note.

"It seems we've blundered into a graveyard after all, Lex. There are books at the hospital, with a complete description. You can make this encounter your scoop for the day."

"Is the border guarded on *both* sides?"

The third guard's eyes had narrowed. He spoke emphatically, with both hands on the stock of his rifle.

"Sorry, *messieurs*. No more questions."

John steered his companion to higher ground, with a firm hand at his elbow. The guardian of the caves had won his argument—and John had good reason to believe he spoke English perfectly. He saw no point in explaining that this was Fa Ngoum, the son of Prince Ngo Singh.

Surprisingly enough, Wilde made no further protest until they had begun their homeward journey. It was apparent that he had accepted the persuasion of the three armed men at face value, and was busy weighing its significance.

"Someone might have warned us," he said at last.

"Unless I'm badly wrong, the presence of those riflemen will be news at the kampong."

"Do you *still* claim things aren't closing in?"

"This is Meo country, Lex. They've every right to police it as they see fit."

"According to that fellow's patter, they're guarding those caves for the *monastery*."

"The Gates are part of the monastery grant: so's the land between. The Prince signed them over long ago."

"I thought he was your friend. How could you get out of bounds so easily?"

"You're the one who's out of bounds, Lex—"

There was no time for more argument, now that the Rover (coasting to the valley floor) had entered the well-worn ruts of the village road. While the jungle had screened them, John had pretended the high-pitched drone held no hint of menace: he could even believe it was the voice of his jet burner, raised at the height of a test run in the not-too-distant laboratory. Now, with open sky above them, he could hardly close his thoughts to that all-embracing sound. Beyond doubting, it came from above, from the engines of a plane.

"Better take cover, John. Just in case."

The advice was sound: Lex Wilde (a veteran of many wars) had seen his share of death from the sky. Swinging the Rover into a bamboo clump at the edge of the village, John vaulted to the road and sought a spot that commanded a full view of the hospital grounds.

"Can you spot a plane, Lex?"

"You always *hear* jets before you see them. I'd say he was coming in from the north."

"There's the vapor trail!"

John pointed to the crest of Butterfly Mountain, where a fat cloud-mass had settled. While they watched, a white-winged, two-engined plane broke through the cover, to bear down on the valley. Matching plumes from its exhausts laid down its course with geometric precision. Already it was evident the pilot was following a familiar sky plot: he had needed no trial run to set his flaps for the Muong Toa airstrip.

"Recognize the silhouette, John?"

"Only the insignia of the Red Cross. It's a hospital plane."

"Our visitor has other markings," said the journalist. "They're much more to the point."

In full view now, the jet was a white shadow against the blue. When it roared above the bamboo thicket, John saw that its pilot had already dropped his wheels for a landing. The red star of China, printed boldly on the fuselage, was a needless reminder of its origin.

# 6.

LATER, when he could pin down his thoughts during that headlong drive to the kampong, John realized that what had shocked him most was the desolation of the village square. The shadow of those wings, it seemed, had cast its spell long before the Chinese plane could level for its landing.

In the marketplace, the stalls were untenanted, though the vendors' baskets still stood on their trestles; in the half-dozen roads that radiated from this focal point, each house was shuttered, and still as death. The compound itself was just as deserted. Only on the airstrip did John detect a sign of life. Here, pilot and copilot had descended from the cabin to stretch their legs. Their jackets were open in the heat of noon: one of them had just lifted a bottle from the ice bucket that stood inside the hangar door. The familiar gesture, John thought (swinging the Land Rover in a prudent arc to avoid the airstrip), could not have seemed more reassuring.

"Are you going to question them, Lex?"

"I wouldn't advise it," said the journalist. "There's Dud Porter. He'll bring us up to date."

The technician had just appeared on the laboratory stoop, with an easy wave of greeting. Dud's calm, like the absence of hostile intent, did much to unwind the knots that gripped John's brain as he stepped from the Rover and moved to join his assistant. Lex remained behind; by Chan's decree, the part of the kampong where Dud stood waiting was out of bounds.

"Don't look so punch-drunk, Boss," said Dud. "There's only *one* visiting fireman here today—name of T. K. Yu. Like you see, the red carpet's out."

The laboratory doors, John saw, were open wide, permitting a glimpse of the first row of worktables: Chan had reacted boldly to the warning of the jet engine.

"Apparently this is a courtesy call," Dud added. "They're visiting in Chinese, so I can't swear I'm right."

"Has Yu seen the convertor?"

"We saw no point in secrecy. When we heard that plane come over, we were running a straight batch of *Thorntoni*—for comparative figures." Dud nodded toward the journalist, who was straining his ears on the far side of the compound. "Unfortunately, the convertor broke down just before they landed. A rupture in one of the main tubes. *Catch*, Boss?"

"I catch," said John. His spirits were growing lighter by the moment.

"Dr. Thornton's sure you'll tell our visitor all you can. We've nothing further to report, have we?"

"Nothing whatever. Does this mean I'm invited to the conference?"

"Chan wants you both in the lab, right away."

"Both of us?"

"Lex has been griping at the lack of news. This could be his way of making amends."

"I still can't take it in, Dud."

"Nor could I, at first. Believe me, Dr. Thornton's running this show his way."

John signaled for the journalist to join them. Wilde stared at him in astonishment while he repeated Dud's tidings.

"Does this mean an unrestricted interview?"

"I doubt if Chan will let you go that far."

"Wrong again," said Dud. "It seems the great man is ready to speak his mind."

Wilde made an impatient start toward the lab, but the microbiologist detained him firmly.

"Promise one thing, Lex. Let Dr. Yu do the talking."

"I'm making no promises. No matter what this fellow says, it's page-one news."

"In Heaven's name why?"

"He's the best of his breed—and he's come here in peace. The Red Cross plane proves that much."

"You said it could be a cover."

"Not when it's unarmed. He's here today as Thornton's

135

friend. Any statement he makes is money in the bank. It's also a perfect follow-up to the views *you* expressed yesterday."

"We don't exchange views with an enemy, Lex."

"Doctors cross battle lines in wartime. Why shouldn't you and the number one nutrition expert of the People's Republic meet halfway?"

From the laboratory door, the scene was innocent enough to disarm the most suspicious observer. Two figures were at the microscope table, each with his eyes fixed to a binocular scope. Chan Thornton's poise, John saw, was too complete to be feigned, and the man from Yunnan seemed entirely at home. When he rose from his seat and bowed to the new-comers, it was easy to forget that he, not they, was the intruder.

Before the change of regimes in China, Dr. T. K. Yu had lectured on his speciality in all parts of the globe. John had seen his photograph a hundred times. Even now, when the famous agronomist was in his late sixties, the plump, aristocratic profile roused a shock of recognition. Both the face and the smile recalled a professor John had once worshiped, a wizard in organic chemistry who treated each student as a son. Like the Chinese agronomist, Dr. Otto von Merz had been bald as an egg and cheerful as a harvest moon. Merely to be in his presence, in lab or classroom, was to grow an inch in stature.

Chan made the introductions in flowing Mandarin. Yu's smile broadened as he offered a graceful gesture of dissent— and spoke in perfect English.

"Since I'm to be interviewed," he said, "I'm sure Mr. Wilde would prefer his own tongue."

"I'll be happy to translate, Doctor."

"English, if you please, Dr. Thornton. I regret my chances to use it are so few."

Noting how the journalist's eyes were roaming the main workroom, John spoke up quickly.

"I'm told this is an unofficial visit, Dr. Yu."

"Entirely, Dr. Merchant."

"Mr. Wilde won't expect an interview in the formal sense. You can hardly talk for the record."

The agronomist made another disarming gesture. "This is a gathering of kindred spirits, gentlemen. Knowing Mr. Wilde, I'm sure he'll report it fairly."

Lex opened his notebook on the microscope table and flung a triumphant glance at John.

"Hunger's your province, Doctor. The record states how hard you've fought it. Do you have hopes of victory?"

Aghast at the boldness of the attack, John opened his mouth to protest, but Yu had already accepted the gambit.

"Hunger has been Asia's first enemy since its history began," he said. "In China, as you know, we've taken desperate measures to control it. Our enemies have called our methods brutal: they say we starve our peasants to improve other aspects of our revolutionary economy. Nothing could be further from the truth. At present, we are facing the aftermaths of crop failure; we must ration what food remains, as best we can."

"Do you expect conditions to improve?"

"When I set up my control centers in Yunnan two years ago, I was far from hopeful. That was before my first visit to this valley. Since then, I have permitted myself a guarded optimism—thanks to Dr. Thornton's own example, and the help he's given me."

Watching Chan narrowly, John could not be sure if he was pleased or startled by the compliment. His features showed only the smile of the model host, to whom a guest's opinions were law.

"Dr. Yu honors me too highly," he said. "The most I've done is donate what food I could spare—and a blight-free rice strain now on file at the World Health Organization."

"The strain has proved its worth in our paddies," said the agronomist. "I won't pretend it's banished hunger, in Yunnan or elsewhere. Our real problems, of course, are played-out soil and the ignorance of those who till it. I do say we've taken the first encouraging steps. My gratitude to *both* Dr. Thorntons is infinite."

"Will these techniques apply to all China?" The question,

137

John realized, was his own. He cast a resentful glance at Lex Wilde's dancing pencil. The journalist had created the mood he desired with his first adroit query—a self-starting discussion that permitted him to supply the interpretation of his choice.

"Unfortunately the approach is unsuited to other areas," said Yu. "Our peasants are slow to learn—and slower still to forget old ways. In time, of course, I hope to control rice blight on a national scale."

"What Dr. Yu has done, so far, is only a beginning," said Chan. "I'm sure he praises me above my deserts. The contributions I made have long since been open to the world."

"Even a beginning is valuable, if it creates a climate of hope," said the agronomist. He turned again to John, and his smile was almost radiant. "Considering your own speciality, Dr. Merchant, I've let myself dream we'll receive help from *you* someday."

"I'm afraid I don't quite follow."

Yu left his stool at the microscope table, and motioned for John to take his place.

"If you will study this slide, it will illustrate my meaning more forcefully than words."

John sat down at the microscope, turning the adjustment with a hand that just escaped trembling. A glance was enough to calm his agitation: this was no hanging drop of the mutation, only a stained smear of his own subspecies, showing a cell division in its simplest form.

"The soil, not the microscope, is my field," said Yu. "But I've training enough to recognize the pure beauty of the organism before you."

"Did you say *beauty?*" Wilde asked.

"Atheists tell us no life endures, Mr. Wilde. As a scientist, I view death as a merging, a renewal: to my mind, nothing is really destroyed in the great scheme of things. The lowly algae are proof that the process is eternal. I might even add it proves the existence of God."

"No biologist could quarrel with your theology," John said. Try as he might, he could not quite match this philosophical

138

blandness. A glance at Chan was reassuring. His friend's cool nod told him the situation was in control.

"Our researchers have observed this simple plant for years," said Yu. "So, of course, have yours. Here at Muong Toa, the study of algal cultures has always had priority. When a man of your stature joined forces with Dr. Thornton, I looked forward to spectacular results."

"It's been a privilege to work with Chan," John said quietly. "We've done our utmost to speed the process you just studied on this gram slide. Our results have been inconclusive." Uttering the lie with aplomb, he turned to the journalist, whose flying pencil had paused at last. "Mr. Wilde has been standing by, in the vain hope of a story. We've had nothing to give him whatever."

"Not even with the last word in solar convertors?"

John glanced casually at the immobile *bat jhow yee*. "It's a useful device. Unfortunately, it can speed nature's rhythms just so far."

"Dr. Thornton tells me it has suffered a breakdown," said Yu. "Can it be repaired? Or will you continue your research in San Francisco?"

"As of now, I'm not sure. My foundation has given me a short leave of absence. Naturally, I can't linger forever."

"It is an open secret that we have these solar convertors in my own country," said the agronomist. "Again I must confess my ignorance of their workings. I do know they will produce edible algal growth when they operate properly. For a time, in fact, we had visions of food to burn."

"To *burn,* Dr. Yu?" Wilde asked.

"I use the verb literally. China needs cheap industrial fuel almost as much as a protein-rich diet. Had our convertors fulfilled our hopes, they might have fed us all—and produced a by-product to feed our hungry factories. The operation remains far too expensive to be practical."

"We reached the same conclusion in the States," said John.

"Even with your own subspecies, the *Chlorella Thorntoni?*"

"It was promising at first. In the end, the same difficulties recurred."

139

"We, too, have run tests with your Chlorella," said Yu. "The reports have been negative—again, largely because of cost."

Pretending to examine the slide a second time, John permitted himself a slight relaxation. He could be sure that Yu's disclaimer was honest.

"Speedup of growth, and its rigorous control, are the two absolutes," he said carefully. "Since you've encountered the same stumbling blocks, I can add nothing to the picture. We've found nature's timetable too strong to challenge. I fear it will remain so."

"The atom-breakers faced similar problems, Dr. Merchant. Eventually they surmounted them: I won't say whether the victory was good or evil. Surely there's no doubting the benefits of your present goal. When I call here next time, I'll hope for better news."

Chan spoke into the silence. "When may I expect you again, Doctor?"

"Not before summer," said Yu. "Until July, at least, I must fight for a banner rice crop: my country's whole future could depend on it. Will you prolong your stay until that date, Dr. Merchant?"

"Perhaps—unless I'm called home by an emergency."

"Can you think of a more compelling task than the one you face here?"

John glanced at Lex, who was still writing madly.

"Before I left my own workroom in the States, I spent seven months on this same problem. Dr. Thornton has recorded over three hundred test runs—all of them self-defeating. No man's patience is infinite."

"Your modesty's becoming," said Yu. "I refuse to accept it. You see, Dr. Merchant, I've read every paper you've published on your speciality. I have also admired your hope of world brotherhood, quoted in Mr. Wilde's last dispatch. Such men as you do not admit defeat."

"How could that column reach you so soon?"

"Mr. Wilde is published regularly in the Hong Kong *Times*. A transcript reached me this morning via the Canton radio. To be honest, it inspired today's flight to Muong Toa."

140

John kept his poker face without too much effort. Instinct told him he was approaching the final hurdle.

"Are you asking if I meant what I said in that column? The answer's a qualified yes. As men of science, I hope we can always talk as brothers. As citizens of hostile nations, our usefulness to each other is limited. It's one of the bitter truisms of our times."

"Today, I ignored those barriers. Suppose I could offer you a real breakthrough on your algae project—with no restrictions on its use. Would you cross into Yunnan to develop it?"

"Of course—if my passport allowed it." Try as he might, John could not quite match the urbanity of Dr. Yu's smile. "Are you making such an offer?"

"Alas no, Doctor. Our scientists' record in this field is even more limited than yours. It is still good to have your answer."

"The hostility of our governments may lessen someday." Aware of the hollow echo in his words, John added a shrug of despair. "Granted, there's little justification for such hopes at present. Algae are puny antagonists compared to the will of man."

"Algae existed before the human brain," said the agronomist. "Other solutions might follow—if we could plumb the secret of their growth, and dominate it."

"It's a point I won't dispute," John said. "May I wish you luck in your own work?"

"The good wishes are accepted," said Yu. "I can use them, considering the tools at my disposal. May *I* wish for a time when we'll be friends, in every sense?" He held out his hand to John, and to Dudley Porter. Then, saluting the still-busy journalist, he bowed deeply to Chan Thornton, and spoke a formal farewell in the language they shared.

Even when he had walked through the open laboratory door and crossed the kampong to enter his waiting plane, it was impossible to doubt the parting wish had been sincere.

Standing at a chink in the shuttered west window, John saw the plane door close and heard the twin jet-engines roar into action. Only when the white wingspan had lifted against

141

the sky did he feel safe in breathing deeply again. Behind him, he heard a heartfelt sigh and knew Dud Porter shared that relief. Only Chan was silent as a stone, as he continued to sit at the head of the worktable, with downcast eyes. It was the correct attitude of abnegation an Oriental host assumes to mark a guest's departure.

Lex Wilde broke the silence. Slapping his notes together, he charged toward the door.

"Censor this story by a comma," he said, "and we'll come to blows."

"The shortwave is yours," said Chan. "I trust your discretion."

John stood aside to let the journalist leave the building. Now that the visitor from Yunnan was only a dot on the horizon, both kampong and hospital had come alive again. On the clinic porch, Dr. Vong appeared, with the caution of a man emerging from the eye of a hurricane. Behind him, a clatter of trays proclaimed a tardy lunch-hour in the ward.

Chan rose at last and dropped the padlock-bars across the outer doors. "The storm has passed on," he said. "It seems we got out of it lightly."

"Will he really stay clear until July?"

"I think we can count on it, John. By the way, that was an excellent bit of acting. I didn't know you possessed such talent."

"Dud told me enough to give me a lead." John turned to check on his assistant. As he had expected, Dud had already gone to the alcove to connect the dismembered tubes. In another instant, the convertor rumbled into tumescent life.

"It was fortunate we had time to set the stage," said Chan. "How did Yu know you had this equipment?"

"His pilot made two passes over the compound. Most of the convertor's visible from the air. Besides, as he told you, they have similar units in China."

"Was it wise, telling Lex so much?"

"My visitor insisted on making a statement of goodwill for the press."

Dud spoke from the alcove. "We stopped with the last

*Thorntoni* run. The mutation's under wraps. So's our new technique with methane."

"Too much secrecy might have spoiled everything," said Chan. "It seemed wiser to throw our doors wide, to insist we had no new findings."

"The big point now is whether Dr. Yu believed us."

"Take my word—he accepted our story, for the present. Of course, he'll go on hoping we're on the brink of a solution."

"If that's his attitude, he may think we're holding back."

"Put it another way, John. He thinks you're a modest genius. Those were his exact words. He feels you're much too cautious to spell out your achievements, until they're in black and white. For those reasons, he'll expect results from that convertor when he makes his next call."

"Does he think we'll share them?"

"I've shared with him before," said Chan. "So did my father."

"Then you really believe he's fighting hunger in Yunnan— and nothing else?"

"I know what's in your mind, of course. To you, he's in the employ of an enemy nation, so you damn him without trial. To me, he's only another dedicated scientist—the sort you endorsed in Wilde's column."

"Speaking of Lex, will you really let his story go un-censored?"

"Why not? He can do us no more harm here. When he was in Bangkok two days ago, he sent a confidential cable to his American editor. He said we were about to announce a great discovery in solar produced food—and promised to cover it."

"How did you learn this?"

"From Dr. Yu himself. *He* was informed by a Thailand agent with access to the cable office. Don't blame him for following up the lead: his people are starving."

"I don't blame him at all," John said slowly. "Nor do I blame Lex. If I were in his place, I'd have sent that cable and tried for another Pulitzer. As a simple-minded American biologist, I'm glad we've covered our tracks. What's more, I'm heading for home tomorrow."

"You're a free agent, John. But can you be sure that's the best solution?"

"It's the only one that's safe. I've already prepared the ground. We can say I was called home by my foundation. I'll finish our job in San Francisco."

"You'd be delayed for months before you could assemble this equipment."

"That's true enough."

"The climate here is ideal for algal culture. With the head start I've given you, we could come up with our answer at any time. How can you think of stopping, when we're on the edge?"

"As an American, it's my duty."

"Because another scientist—a man with a yellow skin—is interested in the result?"

"Surely that's reason enough, when he's our enemy."

Chan dismissed the argument with an impatient gesture— as though he were pushing it bodily aside.

"With a discovery of this size in the making, friends and enemies aren't important!"

The words had been shouted. Silence fastened on the room, while the two men faced each other across a gulf that seemed too wide for leaping.

"Does this mean you'll go on without me?"

"I can't do less, with Dr. Yu on my doorstep."

"How much time will he allow you?"

"You heard him say he plans to return by midsummer. When he does, I'm sure he'll bring his own technicians."

"That gives you less than three months. Forgive my frankness, Chan, but you can't wrap up this equation alone."

"I might, if you'll let Dr. Porter help me."

"Dud's a first-rate biochemist, and he's done wonders for us. He's a technician, not an innovator. I don't think he'll make a further contribution."

"So you consider yourself indispensable."

"Don't you agree, Chan?"

The younger Thornton nodded slowly. "You discovered the subspecies. You isolated it and developed it. My mutation was only a lucky accident. If we're to succeed fully, you must lay down the rules. I still hope we can compromise."

"What did you have in mind?"

Chan hesitated. He was calm enough when he spoke again, though he was still hoarse from his aftermath of anger.

"Let's assume we can begin producing in quantity before the month ends. Why not set up a second convertor—and a third?"

"What would that accomplish?"

"We could run a nutrition test—a real one, this time—using the whole Valley. Dr. Yu will stay clear until the results are in. He didn't interfere before: in fact, his help was invaluable."

"Are you telling me he helped your first diet-check?"

Chan's pause was longer this time, but his eyes did not waver. "I can't say this gracefully, John: all I can do is state the facts. Yu supplied most of the algal powder for that first test."

"Why didn't they run it in China?"

"He couldn't afford rumors that unlimited food was in the offing. It was safer to set up the controls here. When the algal powder proved its value, I knew I was on the right track. Shortly afterward, you announced the discovery of *Chlorella Thorntoni:* that was the next big step forward. My own mutation was the third."

"Are you saying *both* of us launched you—as a specialist in algae?"

"The record bears me out, John."

"And you're using that argument to prove Dr. Yu's entitled to share in our results?"

"You'd use it yourself, if you had an open mind." Chan was shouting again, striding back and forth like a madman. "I know it's too much to expect of you. Go back to the States tomorrow, if you insist. Be a patriot to the end. Take your assistant with you—and a sample of the mutation. Either we're partners all the way, or I'm off the team."

"That's nonsense, Chan. When the results are published, you'd share fully in the credit."

"How could I risk it, once Yu learned we'd lied to him?

By then, our formula would be an American patent. Washington would have locked it in the safe. Or parceled it among its pets—"

"You're making my choice a hard one."

The younger Thornton breathed deep as he struggled for control. When he turned to John again, his manner was almost pleading.

"Promise you'll make no decision until tomorrow."

"I suppose that's fair enough."

"There's one voice you haven't heard—Indra's."

"Why bring her into this?"

"We can hardly avoid it. I want you to talk this whole matter out with her, before you leave Muong Toa. Perhaps you'll end by remaining."

"Surely you don't think *she'll* ask me to stay?"

"Indra knows what I'm fighting to preserve here. You watched the Valley take to earth today when a Chinese plane crossed the mountain. Can you picture it under a foreign yoke —simply because you refused to take my side?"

"What are my alternatives, Chan? Suppose I do stay on— regardless of what I've seen and heard today? Suppose we produce dried algae in quantity—and an equation Dud will accept. Could I take off *then*, without a moment's delay?"

"Of course, John."

"Would you share that equation with Dr. Yu?"

"Who are we, to ask where such a gift would lead? It might mean peace in Asia tomorrow."

"Suppose I can't endorse your optimism—and insist on leaving now? Will you permit me to fly to Chiang Mai in the morning?"

"If that's your choice, I'll fly you there myself."

The argument had reached its crescendo, and its finale. The two friends continued to face one another like spent antagonists who have fought a drawn battle—and realized the futility of prolonging it.

"I'll think over all you've told me—and answer you tomorrow," John said at last.

"You'll talk with Indra first?"

"Yes—and with Prince Ngo Singh."

146

"You won't mind if we continue the current run?"

"Dud is supposed to recharge the convertor in the morning. I'll handle that chore myself, assuming I decide to stay on."

"And if you don't?"

"In that event, we'll refuel the Dakota and hold you to your offer. How long will it remain open?"

"As long as you care to use it, John." Chan's smile was warm again: his quick handclasp dismissed the argument. "I don't think you'll put me to the test."

The microbiologist left the main workroom quickly and turned into the alcove, where the convertor still rumbled over its secrets. Dud Porter, kneeling among the coils to test a plastic sealing, got to his feet with a weary flexing of his muscles.

"Should I ask how things went? Or will you tell me?"

"There's nothing to tell."

"No verdict?"

"So far, it's a hung jury. How much did you overhear?"

"A word here and there. I didn't eavesdrop."

"What would *you* do in my place?"

The assistant let his fingertips rest on a half-distended tube. It had begun to coil and uncoil lazily, like a snake in spring.

"I've been through a lot with this bandy-legged dame, John. I hope we can go down to the wire together."

"With T. K. Yu handicapping the race?"

"Why let that old Chinaman spook you? He doesn't know the old girl's record."

"He'll know it if we're still here on his next visit. Chan says he'll bring in a whole planeload of specialists."

"By summer, we'll be back in Frisco."

"Suppose we're still chasing an equation that adds up?"

"If we are, he'll be the last man on earth to stop us."

"Didn't his visit disturb you at all?"

"Look at this thing in perspective, John. Don't let a problem of ethics foul up a problem of science. The two are like whiskey and chloral hydrate. Taken in moderation, either can give you the illusion you're God. Mix 'em, and you'll find you've swallowed a Mickey Finn."

"So I should stick to my last—as you said last night at dinner?"

"Isn't that the secret of successful living? Suppose Dr. Thornton does kick in with our equation? How long could the Reds make trouble? Don't forget *we'd* be in there pitching too."

"Peiping might become the greatest menace on earth, with a food bomb in its arsenal."

"Not if we beef up our own friends, with the same brand of calories." Dud shrugged as he noted John's black-browed scowl—and turned to pat the steel flank of the convertor. "Hang on to that one fact, Boss: we'll be starting even, and we have the know-how. No one can hog *this* old girl's favors now. She's the whole world's sweetheart."

John found Indra in Chin-ling's garden, pruning a boxwood shaped like a pigmy elephant. There was no need to ask if she had waited there by design.

"Where were you when the plane landed?" he asked.

"In the mission, showing twenty nurses how to tie sutures. We went on with the lesson: it seemed good discipline."

"Evidently it wasn't necessary for *you* to meet our visitor?"

"I've met Dr. Yu before. He's a charming gentleman. So charming, it's hard to remember who he really is."

"I had the same trouble. It's a classic example of the devil's skill in quoting Scripture."

"How much does he know about the convertor?"

While John described his fencing match with Yu—and his long argument with Chan—Indra continued to clip the boxwood with an excellent imitation of composure.

"Were you really *too* surprised by Dr. Yu's call? He was bound to visit us eventually."

John shook his head. Merely by posing the question, she had answered it.

"The Prince prepared me, in a sense," he said. "It's Chan's attitude that shakes me. He *still* thinks he can remain a benevolent neutral and keep his heritage."

"His attitude isn't quite that simple. His mind is Asian.

148

As Asian as Ngo Singh's. Both of them think of evil as a passing phase. In that philosophy, only the good endures."

"Meanwhile, Red China's a reality. Do they think Communism will burn itself out if they are patient? That it will stay inside its own borders?"

"What if they're right?"

"Let's say the gamble pays off. Let's agree that Chan's doing his best to aid all men, regardless of the lunacy of their leaders. That was his father's way—and the way of most earthly saints. I still refuse to believe Papa Oscar would give Dr. Yu the food bomb."

"Not even to preserve his life's work?"

Once more, John felt himself rebound from a blank wall. *Woman is the eternal conserver,* he thought. *Indra, for all her brains, prefers a present reality to a misty tomorrow.*

"Give me a moment to translate your logic," he said. "All of us—you and Chan and I—are trapped by the jinn we're creating. We'll have no peace until we've tamed it to our purpose. Do we agree, so far?"

"The taming will come soon, John."

"Will the jinn *stay* tamed? Will it serve the right people—unless it's surrounded with the proper safeguards?"

"Surely it belongs to all the world."

"You'll agree Washington's part of the world?"

"You'll be taking the equation there, the moment it's complete. You have Chan's promise."

"Will you come too?"

"Of course."

"Would you go back with me—if I left Muong Toa at once?"

"I'm not sure. Please don't force me to a decision."

The torment of her divided loyalty was more than John could bear. Aware that Chan had sent him to this meeting deliberately, knowing he was on the point of yielding, he sought a last, doubtful refuge in compromise.

"We can talk again tomorrow. At the moment, I don't quite know my own mind."

"It's a choice we can't make now, even if we wished. The Dakota will be out of commission—until morning, at least."

"Is this Chan's work—or yours?"

"It's nothing more sinister than a broken fuel pump. They're repairing it now, in the village forge."

"In that case, I've twenty-four hours to battle with my conscience."

Indra was still in the garden when he backed the Land Rover from the garage and headed it toward the monastery. She did not lift her eyes—and her gesture of farewell seemed a forlorn afterthought.

"Call me a patriot if you wish, Your Highness," John said. "It's the way I'm made."

"Surely that isn't a term of reproach, Doctor."

"Samuel Johnson had described patriotism as the last refuge of the scoundrel. I'm sure Chan Thornton would accept the thought."

"And you cannot?"

"I find I must think first of my country—then of the world."

"It's a human failing, Dr. Merchant. Don't reproach yourself for yielding. It takes a true philosopher to see that the whole is greater than the sum of its parts."

"Is that the best advice you can offer me?"

"Are you sure you came to the mountain for advice? Aren't you here to put your personal credo in repair before you leave us?"

The two men were seated in the temple courtyard. Above them, the leaves of the *dracéna,* dancing in a brisk wind, made hectic shadow-patterns on the flagstones. This afternoon, Ngo Singh was muffled in a sheepskin robe. The eyes that studied John beneath the cowl were gentle as ever, and as tolerant.

"Will you blame me too much if I put my country's welfare above all else?" John asked. "Must I give it second place for some larger good I can't see clearly?"

"Think of the future for a moment, Dr. Merchant. Perhaps Johnson's epigram will have meaning, in the long view. Nationalism, like colonialism, may be a dying concept. You could be young enough to observe its demise."

150

"We've never had more new nations than today—or less peace among them."

"Other—and stronger—forces are working to dissolve boundaries," said the Prince. "Your Atlantic Community is an inspiring example. A united Asia could be another—fantastic as the concept seems."

"Under the Red banner?"

"Communism may prevail a while longer. It seems the end of civilization if you refuse to look beyond externals. I hope for a more human solution."

"Unfortunately *my* solution is personal. I can't wait beyond tomorrow to reach it."

"Tell me this, Doctor. Have you ceased to trust your friend's judgment of what's best for the Valley?"

John lifted his face to the wind, in a vain effort to wipe the cobwebs from his mind.

"Whether I trust Chan or not, I feel it's madness to continue our experiments."

"You say you've been granted a breathing spell. Won't it be sufficient?"

"He means to inform Dr. Yu when the breakthrough comes. He feels he must tell Yu everything, to save the Valley."

"He has also promised to guarantee you possession of the equation, a batch of mutation culture, and transport to Thailand. Do you question that promise?"

"Not for a moment."

"Can you expect more from a shared enterprise?"

"Would *you* surrender the process to Dr. Yu?"

"I think I would," said the Prince, "if it kept the peace in Asia."

"Then you'd go on as before, in my place?"

"You and Chan have worked well together. Why not stay a little longer, until the pattern of events is clearer? Suppose you desert your best friend tomorrow—and take this half-finished work to America. Suppose Communist guerrillas occupy this valley and wipe out the Thornton image. Could you endure your sense of guilt, if you helped to bring that about?"

"The last time I was here, you told me Chan had no right to surrender the equation—unless I consented."

Ngo Singh offered his most baffling smile. "Didn't you give that consent this afternoon, before you left the laboratory?"

"It's true that Chan feels he's won me over. In *his* mind, there's no question of the decision I should reach."

"Is there a doubt in yours?"

The microbiologist turned away without replying. The canker of rebellion persisted, despite that apparent surrender.

"I'd give all I possess, if I could stay on with a clear mind," he said at last.

"You'll sleep on your decision, I gather?"

John smiled wanly, with his eyes on the silhouette of Butterfly Mountain. "Chan will give me that much time."

"Stay here again, if you like. We can talk in the morning."

"I've presumed enough on your patience. In any case, I must be at work early."

"Does this mean your tests are to continue?"

"Unless I decide to end them. If I reach that conclusion, I'll send you word."

"Please do," said the Prince. "This project of Chan's has always been close to my heart."

"And to mine, until today."

Ngo Singh opened the monastery gate, and offered his hand.

"Perhaps that feeling will return. For humanity's sake, I pray it does."

"Humanity's a concept I find hard to grasp at this moment."

"Keep trying, Doctor. For all his faults, man deserves a second chance."

It was time to leave the sanctuary of Gautama Buddha, to face his private furies in solitude—but John lingered a moment longer in the shadow of the gateway. A bizarre memory had risen to his mind, and he voiced it without pausing to weigh its meaning.

"If you trust the human race, why do you post guards at the caves below the Gates? Do *you* have a secret you can't share?"

152

It was the first time he had seen the Prince disconcerted. Ngo Singh recovered his composure quickly.

"Are you suggesting a philosopher should practice what he preaches?"

John shrugged. "I accepted your son's reason for excluding me. He said the caves were sacred to the dead."

"The reason's as good as any other," said the Prince. "Let us forget the dead for now. The power you hold in your hand belongs to the living. Try to bestow it wisely."

When he wakened, John was astonished to find he had overslept. For the first time that week, he had opened his eyes to a personal universe in perfect repair. His conscience was at peace: the turmoil of indecision that had possessed his waking thoughts had given way to a larger tranquillity— the sure knowledge that he could tame Chan's *bat jhow yee* before the day ended.

He rehearsed the taming process one more time while he slipped into his work clothes. The phenomenon of his inspiration was a familiar one, and it had served him well before: his subconscious mind had labored while he slept, absorbing pieces of information from higher levels, as deftly as a computer devours the elements of a problem that at first glance seems insoluble. The answer had been found—somewhere between dark and dawn.

His personal problem remained, but there was no time to face it now. *Come what may,* he told himself, *you must stay on until Indra is ready to leave Muong Toa.* Until she had made her own decision, he would simply play for time and trust Chan's promise to speed their departure.

In the dining room, he found Dud Porter dozing over a coffee cup.

"Don't jump on me, Boss," said his assistant. "I've forgotten how to sleep by normal means."

"Didn't Chan relieve you at midnight?"

"I sent him about his business. He was discouraged enough to go quietly."

"Is the convertor still charged?"

Dud shook his head. "It's been flushed out thoroughly. I

153

stood over the technicians to make sure." He yawned prodigiously, and tottered to his feet. "Want me to give it a fresh meal, now you're taking over?"

"I'll charge it myself. And don't show your face in that lab until you're really rested."

When John's breakfast had arrived from the kitchen, he sat for a long time at the table—unaware of the food before him while he made his final sketches. The plan born during the night had built steadily: until he had proved its worth in the laboratory, he knew it would be pointless to discuss its details. When he glimpsed Lex Wilde emerging from the guest bungalow, he left the dining room in haste, via the hospital kitchen. Entering the lab by his usual route, he went to the alcove with a fast beating heart. It was not until he had locked the panels behind him that his mind closed on his blueprint.

Pumped clean of its culture medium, with its furnace banked and its tentacles flaccid, the convertor had lost its sinister aura. Taking a leaf from Dud's book, John could not resist an impulse to address the now-impotent monster directly.

"You've fought me a long time, my friend," he said. "Today, you'll begin taking orders, or I'll have your heart."

He had already opened a cabinet to extract a pair of shears and a ball of tough cording. These tools he carried into the court, where he paced off the length of each major tentacle. Then, returning to the convertor, and using a rule-of-thumb measure, he began tying off the tapping tubes Dud had attached to the first portions of the solar segments. It was a laborious process, not too different from a surgeon's ligation of blood vessels, and his muscles ached when he rose to his feet again. Moving outward from the *bat jhow yee,* and covering two-thirds of each major tube, the discharge of methane to the gas burner was now cut off completely. The balance of each tentacle would continue to supply its quota as before.

A last, even more vital chore remained, and John performed it promptly. At the spot where the tapping tubes remained untied, he slit the plastic wall of each tentacle, lifted out the small, heavily perforated tube that supplied

154

carbon dioxide, and tied it off firmly. The procedure would stop further flow of $CO_2$ to the last segments of the solar tubing.

Engrossed in his task, he had lost track of time. A knock on the panel recalled him to the present while he was tying off the last carbon dioxide feeder. He choked down a curt dismissal when he recognized Indra's voice. This, in the truest sense, would be the climax of their long testing. It was right that she should witness it.

"I didn't mean to seem exclusive," he said as he slid the panels open. "I was only preparing a surprise for Dud."

Indra circled the convertor in wide-eyed astonishment. "What's your plan—to cripple the whole operation?"

"On the contrary. I'm trying to give our octopus a new lease on life." John moved to the supply cabinet to bring out a stack of plastic patches and the cement Dud used to repair breaks in the tubing.

"Chan's about to make a pickup at the border," Indra said. "Shall I tell him what you've done?"

She had turned to the door—but he stopped her, with a hand on her shoulder.

"Believe me, I'm *not* destroying our Frankenstein," he said quietly. "Give me a moment more, and I'll show you it's a friend of man." He knelt beside the nearest of the tentacles and began spreading a patch over the slit he had just made. Indra hesitated—then knelt beside him.

"I thought Chan had a corner on mysteries," she said. "Apparently this is turnabout."

"What I've done is simple enough," John assured her. "Essentially, it's the process we've followed from the start. I'm merely attacking from another angle."

"By closing the inner tubes and denying carbon dioxide to the last third of the culture?"

John chuckled—and moved on to seal another slit in the plastic. "I *thought* you'd grasp the point—when you realized this wasn't sabotage." Leaving Indra to finish the job of sealing, he circled the convertor to check the vat of culture medium the technicians had prepared that morning. "I haven't mentioned the cream of the jest. My inspiration came direct from yesterday's visitor."

"From *Dr. Yu?*"

"We were discussing techniques of solar conversion. He said we'd have food to burn if we could devise some way to harvest dried algae cheaply. Food to *burn,* mind you—a source of industrial fuel."

"It's a logical wish," said Indra. "Coal was once plant growth."

"Exactly. And the solution of our whole problem is embedded in those words."

"I'm still in the dark."

"So was I, until this morning. Somehow, the words stuck in my mind while I slept. As you observe, they've produced a significant change in the convertor. Shall I repeat the facts we've established so far? Even though you know them by heart?"

"I think you'd better, John."

"First, we know Chan's mutation is capable of unlimited, explosive growth. Unfortunately, its life cycle drowned itself in methane. So he couldn't harvest above a certain figure—"

"You don't have to go back *that* far!"

John ignored the girl's cry of impatience. "Siphoning off the methane with those tapping tubes was some help. So was our stepped-up infusion of $CO_2$. We were still attempting the impossible: to achieve a balance between growth and decomposition. Do you remember enough college science to state the Law of Mass Action?"

Watching Indra intently, he saw the first gleam of comprehension in her eyes.

"Doesn't it define the physical absolutes that control all chemical reactions?"

"It also diagnoses the digestive pains in our monster. We'll never find an equation for maximum production until we remember we have food to burn in these plastic coils—*and burn it.*"

"Literally?"

"Yes, Indra. Instead of letting two processes cancel each other out, we're turning a basic law to our advantage. We're

156

about to burn part of our Chlorella growth—enough to furnish the carbon dioxide our cells need. And we'll do it in the simplest way—by letting enough methane form to provide carbon dioxide by combustion."

"I'm still a step behind you."

"Look at each of those tentacles. You'll see I've tied off all the tapping tubes on their first sections."

"What biologists call the proximal portion?"

John nodded. "Since those segments are closest to the convertor pump—and the main tube from the furnace—we can supply them with enough carbon dioxide to provide an ideal growth-pattern. Here we'll have maximum cell division with *no* formation of methane. In the far ends of the tubes, the last third, I've cut off the $CO_2$ completely, to produce *nothing* but methane. We'll draw this into the jet burner as before, forming added charges of carbon dioxide for our culture in the proximal portions. Are you with me now?"

"I think so. By dividing the two processes, we'll have food to eat—and food to burn."

"That's it, Indra. At the proximal end where growth's occurring at top speed, we'll have enough $CO_2$ to hold the tempo. Here, for the first time in its short life, Chan's mutation can set its own pace. At the far end of each tentacle, well out of the way of our growth-process, another portion of our culture will be *dying* at top speed. As it dies, it will pump methane into the circuit, supplying the energy to make the life cycle complete."

"How can you keep the methane production in hand?"

"Dud can solve that problem easily by removing most of the adult cells—and leaving just enough to supply the fuel we'll need. If we get too much methane, we harvest a bit faster. Too little, and we cut down on the amount we send to the centrifuges."

"It works out on paper, John. Will it work in fact?"

"I've told you the *bat jhow yee* is straining at the leash. After its spotty record to date, it's eager to prove it can deliver."

John had expected the next hour to be a time of singing triumph. Actually, the charging of the apparatus, the first firing of the ovens, and the familiar, hectic throb of the tentacles proceeded almost without conscious planning.

It was only with the first formation of methane—when the culture had begun to flow into the last still-flaccid solar sections, and the whine of the jet burner told him the gas was moving freely through the tapping tubes—that he felt his heart turn over.

Thanks to that added combustion, it seemed only a heartbeat more until the rich charge of $CO_2$ (ideally concentrated for the first time) began to pour into the proximal portion of the convertor. A prodigal bubbling was already churning the culture to a froth, spinning the swiftly reproducing Chlorella cells in endless revolutions, giving them maximum exposure to the life-giving sun. With Indra at the pressure gauge, the microbiologist continued to circle the outer court, making notes on the rate of accumulation in the tapping tubes. The jet burner, tuned to concert pitch, seemed willing to continue its whine forever. When its hungry sound diminished at last, John lifted one hand palm outward. It was time to begin the crucial harvesting.

When he re-entered the control room, Indra had already begun to draw off the greenish, milky liquid into the settling tank. At her nod, John threw in the centrifuge switch to complete the processing for their first load. Again their hands moved in well-rehearsed tasks, bringing extra drying-trays to take the original harvest, opening the vents to speed the process of dehydration.

Neither of them spoke again while they waited for the oven to complete their task. Indra's only concession to the torment of waiting was a quick move to the scales. The bar was already set at the maximum yield attained so far in their test runs.

"How many kilos shall I add, John?"

"Use your own judgment. Our friend has performed nobly."

He did not dare glance at the stack of weights she placed on the scale. When he opened the doors of the dryer, and brought the trays to the weighing platform, he continued to keep his eyes on Indra's, letting his spirits catch fire from their sudden, exultant gleam.

158

When the girl spoke the new figure, her voice was only a whisper. He made the notation with a trembling hand, then turned to sift a pinch of the hot greenish powder through his fingers.

"Can you believe it, John?"

"Of course. It's a simple biochemical demonstration, nothing more. The mutation is the determining factor. The end product is Food Unlimited."

"You really mean *unlimited,* don't you?"

"You saw it with your own eyes. What's more, this was only a *test* run. When Dud puts the apparatus in a foolproof harness, the process will deserve its name."

"Don't you feel like a man who discovered a gold mine?"

"That and more, Indra," he said quietly. "I've won an even greater treasure."

Even before she could move into his embrace, he knew she had grasped his meaning fully. Now that the formula had arranged itself as neatly as a Q.E.D. in freshman geometry, their work was ended. There would be no need to linger in Muong Toa for Dud Porter's detailed recapitulation of what had already been proved: in a matter of hours, his nimble assistant would imprison their findings in an ironclad mathematical equation any scientist could read. Forged at last by the mutation of *Chlorella Thorntoni,* the food bomb was real as the sunlight that poured down on this maze of solar tubes.

Lost in each other and the heady wonder of success, John and Indra were hardly aware of the discreet cough from the alcove doorway. It was only when the sound changed to a wolf whistle that they broke apart. Dud Porter came in briskly, polishing his glasses as he moved toward the tray-burdened scales.

"Is *this* where you two have been doing your necking?" he asked. "I might have guessed."

Indra moved toward the worktable, with only the faintest of blushes.

"Look at that scale, Dr. Porter," she said. "You'll see why we're celebrating."

"Read my notes while you're about it," John added. "They'll make your eyes pop out."

"They're popping now," said Dud. He was already staring at the scale, and the towering stack of trays, each heaped with its quota of powder. "Was it sporting to hold out on me, Boss?"

"Dr. Yu's the hero of this final skirmish, Dud. We'd be hitting the same stone wall, if he hadn't called on Chan yesterday."

Dud did not speak while John repeated the story of the last test run, and the planning that had preceded it. Then he bent above the *bat jhow yee*, to kiss the still-warm metal. "And to think the gimmick was right under my nose all the time," he said mournfully.

"We can still thank T. K. Yu for supplying it."

"I'll send him a postcard from San Francisco, Boss. Now we're home free, I won't say I'm surprised. I always figured this old girl would deliver eventually. I'll grant you, she *was* flighty as an ingenue at times."

"She was a faithful servant. We just didn't grasp her needs."

Dud moved briskly across the alcove to check the empty culture vat.

"Shall I put her to work again, now she's had her breather?"

"By all means. You'll want comparative figures on the new growth-section. We may have made this first one too short."

"A few more runs will give us all we need, John. Three at the outside, I'd say. There's sunlight to spare for that."

Indra had already gone toward the incubators. "I'll bring a fresh flask of mutation."

"Leave that job to me, Miss Lal. When I came in just now, I was so bowled over I forgot I had a message. Dr. Vong wants you in the clinic."

John and Indra exchanged a startled look. Engrossed as they had been in the finale of their experiment, they had half-forgotten the world outside.

"Did he say what he wanted?"

"Another cholera case has come in. Don't ask me to pronounce the name of the village."

"Was it Phong Kal?"

"I think so."

"It's a herdsman's pasture on the mountain. They always

put off their booster shots. So cholera hits them hard when it strikes."

"If you're giving them the needle," said Dud, "I'd suggest you take John for company. He deserves a half-day off while I wind this up."

John considered. The idea of a breather was attractive—and a journey to the mountain might give him time to report to Prince Ngo Singh.

"Sure you can handle the monster alone?"

"A robot could run the next test with your data-sheet," said Dud. "If you like, we can wrap up the package today."

"Today will do nicely."

"What shall I tell Dr. Thornton—if he beats you back to the kampong?"

"Only that I'm holding him to his promise."

In the clinic dispensary, John and Indra picked up the kits Oscar Thornton had devised for emergency medication in the hills. They contained ampules of cholera vaccine, syringes, and a portable fish-kettle sterilizer where the needles could be boiled. There were bottled antibiotics, for use in immediate drug prophylaxis. Dr. Vong, as always, had included sacks of hard candy, a standard bribe that would induce both adults and children to bare their arms for the injection.

Indra detoured to the nurses' wing while John carried the kits to the second Land Rover. Ten minutes later, she emerged in windbreaker, jodhpurs, and knee-high walking boots. Binoculars were slung at her shoulder, along with a mapcase.

"I see you haven't forgotten anything," he said.

"Only my common sense, John. We can still ask Dr. Vong to go in our place."

"Why should we? Dud won't need us: he was right when he said a robot could wrap up the equation."

"What about Mr. Wilde?"

"Lex can have his interview later—when Dud closes his notes."

It was sheer delight to roll through the kampong gates without a twinge of conscience for work undone, to feel the powerful lift of the Rover's engine on the first steep grades of the mountain road. John offered no objection when they sped past the monastery gate, to negotiate the higher slopes: this was their last day in Muong Toa, and they had every right to set their own pace. The visit to Ngo Singh, he promised himself, would come on the way back.

For the next hour, the car followed a series of hairpin curves that lifted them far above the Valley—until the road entered a grove of wind-twisted cedars just below timberline. Here the rough trace seemed to end entirely, but Indra (after a glance at her map) sent their transport careening into the cropped grass that lay beyond.

"If my bump of direction's accurate," John said, "this meadow is just behind the north face of Butterfly Mountain."

"It's as close as we dare go. Chan tells me they've had several rockslides above. He thinks they were caused by the blasting in Yunnan." Indra let the Rover coast to a stop below a brush-choked cliff that bounded the field on the west. Here, a dogleg path mounted to the summit, and a second, boulder-strewn meadow.

"*This* trail looks chancy enough," John said.

"It isn't really dangerous. Have you done much climbing lately?"

"Dud and I worked in the Rockies last fall—on an outbreak of bubonic plague in ground squirrels. Since then, I've managed to keep in fair condition at Squaw Valley."

"What did you do there—put down an Indian uprising?"

"It's a skiers' paradise near San Francisco. We'll visit it, once this business is behind us."

"Today, it seems as far off as Dr. Yu."

The ascent of the bluff was less difficult than it seemed. The higher meadow, John found, sloped to a chasm he recognized as the gorge of the Hou, a river that descended in a series of cataracts to the valley floor. Most of the slope had been burned over and seeded with poppies. The opium flower (the Meo's chief source of income) was just bursting into bloom. The foundation poles of an abandoned village stood on the far side of the gorge, joined to the meadow by a crude bridge. A seminomadic people, the Meo believed too long a sojourn in any spot was a hazard to health. Their custom was

162

to move along these mountain ridges, burning the land at each transfer to assure another yield of opium.

"At least they've left a bridge to their poppy field," John said. "It must mean they put a little trust in the future."

A closer view of the span (tossed, like an overgrown creeper, across the gorge) did nothing to slow his heartbeat. It was a thing of bamboo, innocent of handrails and secured to boulders by a mesh of leather thongs that seemed far too frail to sustain a man's weight. He stifled a gasp when Indra, stepping on the flimsy flooring as lightly as a chamois, reached the far side in a dozen easy strides. Forcing himself to follow, he was careful not to look below, where the Hou tumbled toward the valley in a remote thread of silver. Midway of the crossing, there was an ominous creak: it warned him that the span would support no greater weight. An ax-stroke would be enough to isolate these tribesmen from enemies below.

Indra gave him a hand at the far side. "I'd forgotten the sheltered life you'd been leading," she teased.

"Do I look as frightened as I feel?"

"We can rest a moment if you like."

"I wouldn't hear of it."

The next crest marked the true beginning of the timber-line. Here a dozen goats grazed on the sparse grass. The trail wound ever upward, toward a notch where a herdsman, perched like a living scarecrow, watched their approach impassively. When Indra signaled with her medical kit, the man rose (a move that revealed a carbine and crossed bandoliers beneath his ragged cloak) and stood aside to let them pass.

The pantomime was repeated twice in the next steep mile. Finally the path spiraled round a rock spur, to end in a grassy hollow that seemed to hang suspended in the sky. Just under its rim, a score of wattled huts stood on spider-legged supports, with a plot of garden before each doorway. Obviously the sentinels had signaled a warning of their approach: the entire village waited outdoors to greet the visitors.

At first glance, thanks to their quilted smocks and trousers, men and women seemed almost identical. Without exception, they were wiry and extremely dark, blending with their

163

rugged environment as naturally as the goats they tended. As always, John found himself warming to the dogged courage that had preserved the identity of the Meo over the centuries, enabling them to face the worst trials nature had to offer. Men of this stripe, he told himself, would outlast any invader from the lowlands, and disdain his orders to the end.

Without quite knowing why, he found himself holding back while Indra exchanged ceremonial greetings with the headman. Muong Toa was far below them now, but it had been a fallacy to pretend he could put it from his thoughts, merely by changing from scientist to mountaineer.

He could still see each detail of the lab with merciless precision, as clearly as though he stood beside the panting convertor. Try as he might, he could not ignore the images his racing mind had formed, when the process they had leashed that morning went into gear. Blown to giant size, duplicated by the hundreds, Chan's *bat jhow yee* could change the folkways of the Meo overnight. Was he a traitor to his calling when he wondered if the change would make these nomads happier?

He shook off the heresy and stepped forward to grasp the headman's hand.

The threat that had brought them to the mountain was less serious than Indra had feared. Actually, they found only three cases of sickness in the village—all of them suspect rather than actual cholera. The headman, nevertheless, had prepared for the worst. A quarter-hour after the arrival of the two *médecins* from the Valley, he had assembled his entire flock before the hut he had chosen as a dispensary.

Since the inhabitants of Phong Kal were overdue for booster shots, John and Indra laid out their ampules on the trestle the headman had provided and inoculated their charges to the last toddler. As an added precaution, the three suspect cases were given heavy doses of tetracycline- -and a supply of the drug was left behind, to treat others who might become ill before the vaccine could lift their immunity to a safe level. When the task was completed, the visitors adjourned to the headman's house for the rice wine that always ended such

164

visits. The sun was still high when they began their return journey.

At the cleft where they had met the first herdsman, the goats had drifted to other pasture, but the sentry-post was still tenanted. At a distance, the figure in the tattered cloak seemed identical. When the man rose to detain them, John saw it was Fa Ngoum, the son of Prince Singh. Even before they could exchange the set phrases of greeting, there was something in the young man's face that sent his spirits plummeting.

"My father saw you pass the temple gates, Doctor. He had planned to send a message to the village. When he learned you were ascending the mountain, he sent me here to await you."

"What is the noble Prince's message?"

"He wishes you to return by a different route."

"As always, I am at the Prince's orders."

"With your permission, I will speak with the lady. She knows the trail."

John did not stir while Indra joined Ngoum in the notch. Their conference was long, and it involved a careful consultation of her map. Twice, he saw her shake her head in disbelief. When she returned to the path, her lips were set in a thin line.

"Ngo Singh wishes us to use the high trail. His son tells me it's passable again. The Meo have cleared away the worst of the rockslides."

"Is that all he told you?"

"Let's forget the rest, until we've followed through."

Turning to plunge uphill in a shower of falling gravel, she gave John no time to question her: there was a curtness in the move that discouraged conversation, even if the climb had left him breath to spare.

For the next half-mile, the trail was plainly marked, a knife-thin path that snaked below the last, steep escarpments of Butterfly Mountain. Here and there, small avalanches had all but engulfed it, but it was still possible to detour. Both of them were panting when they paused to draw a bead on their

165

next objective—a flat ledge that seemed to hang above the same gorge they had crossed at early afternoon.

"Can't you give me *some* idea of what we're after?"

Indra kept her eyes on the terrain above. The question, he knew, had been futile.

"We're having a look at China, John. The Prince thinks we'll find it revealing."

He made no attempt to press her. Conscious that she was the leader of this bizarre journey (and aware that she could outclimb him with ease), he followed her across the gorge on another slatted bridge that seemed as frail as the first.

"You said this was a short cut to Muong Toa," he reminded her at last.

"It is. You can see the Valley now."

She had pointed downhill as she spoke, and he saw they were directly above the meadow where they had left the Rover. Ahead, no more than a few hundred feet higher, a knife-edge of granite cut off the northern sky.

"Why didn't we come this way, Indra? It isn't dangerous."

"Chan advised against it. I . . . followed his advice."

"And now you've taken your bearings from the Prince?"

"Yes, against my better judgment. Stay where you are, please. I'm going to take a look from that *sérac* above us. We mustn't let ourselves be seen."

Indra ascended the slope in a series of agile bounds that left John breathless. At the summit, just below the knife-thin ridge, he saw her flatten to hands and knees, unlimber the binoculars, and peer down the northern face of the mountain. Disregarding her warning (now he had grasped her purpose), he followed at a more cautious pace. Like her, he dropped to hands and knees below the ridge, then joined her in the cleft she had chosen as an observation post.

"Keep your head down," she said tonelessly. "We can't be too careful."

Her voice had broken on the words; her body was shaken by a sob, as she turned away from what she had just seen and thrust the binoculars into his hands. There was an urgency in the move that wiped all other considerations from his mind.

A moment later, with the glass adjusted to his vision, he swept the northern face of the mountain and the jungle-choked reach below. His first quick glance was enough to reveal the peril they were facing.

# 7.

THE geography of the region had fallen into place with the first sweep of the binoculars. The ledge where John and Indra lay—a part of the long crest of Butterfly Mountain—was a mile distant from the western pinnacle of the Gates of Hell. Thanks to the proximity of the Land Rover, the hospital kampong (lost, at that moment, in the cloud cover of the Valley) was under an hour's drive away. Making these estimates automatically, John turned again to the north, and the facts the high-powered glasses had revealed.

The Chinese face of the mountain was somewhat less precipitous than the slopes facing Muong Toa. Here and there, where teak forest blended with jungle, quarries had been carved out boldly: at that height, they stood out like livid scars against the green. It was here that the engineers in Yunnan had found the raw material for their project. Obviously, continual blasting had started the rockslides at the summit, on both sides of the mountain.

The project itself lay less than ten miles beyond. Studied with the naked eye, it would have seemed only a larger scar on the landscape. Brought into focus by the binoculars, it told its own story. What Chan had called a power dam was actually a road, whose purpose was grimly apparent even to the layman's eye. Winding from the heat-hazed forest to the north, it grew arrow-straight as it approached the cleft beyond the mountain. Here, it pointed for the Gates, and Oscar Thornton's Valley.

The engineering feat, considering the terrain, was formi-

167

dable. The binoculars told John this was an all-weather highway. Once it reached the Gates, it would descend to the valley by the easiest of grades: buttressed by those tons of crushed stone from the mountain, it would compare with the finest macadam. The work force that swarmed down its dusty length was efficient as an ant platoon, and almost as numerous. Droves of coolies were swarming at the dump trucks, queuing at the rockcrushers, spreading hot tar on the highway surface, or dragging the rollers that completed the tamping.

Among the workers in the quarries, which were much nearer to where they lay, John recognized dozens of turbaned Kha (as always, the workhorses of the area, whose brute loyalties could be secured for a pittance). Here and there, he noted uniformed sentinels. A command post, rising on makeshift stilts, clung precariously to the side of the roadway, at a point where its inexorable thrust southward met the wall of jungle. He could almost be sure that these were regulars (in the uniform of the People's Republic) rather than local militia.

So far as he could estimate, no more than two miles of uncut timber lay between the Gates and the point of the enemy arrow. An apron of rocky plain outlined the creekbed that watered the defile—and the faint trace that had been the only link between Muong Toa and the country to the north. Somewhere in that powder-white bustle, John knew, was the Chinese border.

"Ngo Singh hears they'll finish blasting before the summer ends," said Indra. "By fall, they mean to pierce the Valley."

Her voice seemed to reach John from a great distance. Turning from his reconnaissance, he forced himself to answer calmly.

"When was the Prince informed?"

"This morning, when his son returned. Fa Ngoum dressed as a Kha and joined a road gang."

John lifted the binoculars for a last incredulous look. He remembered his talk with Ngo Singh, and the son's calm acceptance of the risks involved in a sortie to Yunnan.

168

"How could they progress this far without the Prince knowing?"

"The Meo are forbidden to enter Chinese territory: Fa Ngoum was the first to break the taboo. He'd heard of the road from a captured Pathet Lao soldier. Last week, he crossed the border to check the story."

*Chan* thought they were building a power dam."

"How could he think that? He'd driven to the checkpoint a score of times."

"Perhaps he never saw the construction itself."

"You know better, John, and so do I."

Pretending to concentrate on the mountain's north face, the microbiologist did not answer. So far, he had not dared to meet Indra's level stare.

"Shouldn't we give him a chance to explain?"

"What's left to explain now?"

"The Prince himself has just learned the truth. Why should Chan be better informed?"

"Because he's one of them. He's been one of them for a long time. Why not admit it?"

"It's a hard fact to face, Indra."

"He's covered his tracks from the start—and done it brilliantly. When he warned us to keep off the mountain because of rockslides, he *must* have known what caused them."

John restored the binoculars to their case, as they continued to crouch (like two secret agents) in their rock cleft.

"I won't deny the evidence is damning—"

"It's obvious they mean to take over the Valley before the year's out," the girl said quickly. "It may be an entering wedge for a move on southeast Asia."

"And Chan knew all along? Is that what you're saying?"

"The Prince is sure of it. He wants you to leave at once—to take this news to the American command in Saigon." Indra's voice had finally steadied. "And he hopes you'll forgive him for urging you to stay."

"If what he thinks is true, can we get out so easily?"

"We can try. There's enough daylight left to reach Chiang Mai in the Dakota."

"What about the *bat jhow yee?*"

"Chan can have that. It won't matter if we take the mutation cultures with us. Remember, only Dr. Porter has the complete equation. It's all the head start you'll need."

Their descent to the valley floor was made in record time. On the last steep turn, John considered the wisdom of pausing for consultation with the Prince, only to resist the idea. Time was precious now, if they meant to take off by daylight.

In the outskirts of the village, Indra cut the Rover's speed. From this point, they had agreed, they must move slowly, in case they were observed by hostile eyes. John could find nothing sinister in the drowsy quiet of the kampong. At his request, the girl drove the car into the hospital garage, where they paused deliberately to give a houseboy instructions for a battery check. Then (forcing himself to stroll) he followed Indra to the pergola, where they paused to make their final plans.

"I must change into uniform," the girl said. "It might seem odd if I don't."

"Who shall I tell first—Dud or Lex?"

"Mr. Wilde, if he's in the guesthouse. If not, you must go straight to the lab and take out what you need. I'll slip down to the hangar to see if the plane's operable."

"Is there a chance it won't be?"

"I stopped at the forge this morning and asked them to hurry the pump. If it's installed, we can take off as soon as I refuel."

"Suppose the plane's still grounded?"

"In that case, I'll join you and Dr. Porter."

"I don't like leaving you this way."

"We've no option. I know it's hard, but we must behave as though nothing had happened."

There was no sign of Dr. Vong when John took the shortcut through the men's ward, to enter the guest bungalow by the back door. Lex Wilde's room was empty, though an overflowing ashtray beside the typewriter testified to the journalist's recent presence. A glance through the window (which commanded a view of the airstrip) told John that

170

Indra was already returning from the hangar. She was moving at a snail's pace, and the droop of her shoulders was a chilling admission that the mechanics (perhaps on orders from Chan) had soldiered on their job.

Setting his pace to Indra's—and waiting deliberately until she had entered the lab—John crossed the kampong, paused to exchange a few words with the houseboy at work in Chin-ling's garden, then circled the west wing of the hospital to approach the lab in turn. He was rocked on his heels when he saw Chan's Land Rover parked at the clinic porch.

Again, both padlocks were down in the laboratory vestibule and the doors were flung wide. From the entrance, John could identify the murmur of Chan's voice, punctuated by an occasional query from Lex Wilde: it was obvious the younger Thornton was dictating a statement on the morning's breakthrough. His measured tone, and the hum of the convertor, were the only sounds to break the silence. Half-expecting to collide with Dr. Yu, John was relieved to find no one present but his team—and the journalist.

The group had gathered in the alcove. Indra sat a little apart from the others, with a notebook on her knee. Dud, with one foot in the courtyard, lifted two locked hands in greeting, like a prizefighter celebrating a knockout. The gesture set the final seal on the tableau. So did the tall stacks of drying-trays beside the scales, each brimming with its quota of greenish powder.

"As you see, John, I returned early," said Chan. "There were no casualties at the checkpoint. In the circumstances, I felt I should fulfill your bargain with Mr. Wilde. You'll forgive us for proceeding without you?"

The younger Thornton, John observed, had assumed his usual regal manner, as naturally as his lab coat. Accepting his cue without effort, he chose a stool not too far from Indra.

"Can I add anything to the picture?"

"I think not," Chan said. "Dr. Porter had briefed me thoroughly: I'm sure my presentation has been adequate."

John glanced round the table. Indra's nerves, he saw, were in firm control: so far, no mind but his own had read the meaning of her troubled glance.

"I hope you kept back the technical details," he said.

"You can trust me there, John." Chan's face glowed with triumph—but his voice was almost gentle now, filled with a humility that was strangely moving. "Mr. Wilde knows that those details are shared by four people only: you, Dr. Porter, Miss Lal and myself. We regard them as a priceless possession."

The journalist spoke, with his eyes on his shorthand notes. It was only when John caught the tremor in his voice that he realized the depth of Wilde's excitement.

"Shall I read back what you've given me?"

"Please do," said Chan. He had spoken as quietly as before, but the note of authority was unmistakable.

"I'll skip my lead paragraphs and give you the essence." Skimming his notes with a practiced eye, Wilde turned to the third page, and began to read his story—as smoothly as though he were dictating to a teletypesetter in his New York office:

Prior to the work of Dr. Thorton's international team, the growing of algae for food had reached a virtual impasse. Average yields, even at the best experiment stations in America and Europe, were no better than seventeen plus tons per acre of culture area.

The end product, since it was fifty percent protein, was a virtually perfect food, requiring practically no supplement for a fully adequate diet. Unfortunately, costs were still prohibitive, compared to the ordinary harvests of such staples as corn, wheat or rice.

When the new test runs began at Muong Toa, optimum results had been achieved with a culture medium called *Chlorella Thorntoni*, an algal subspecies discovered and isolated by Dr. Merchant. A mutation of this subspecies was later developed by Dr. Thornton in his Muong Toa laboratory—using a still-secret technique to insure what biologists call "true breeding." Its feature was a runaway growth-rate that can only be called phenomenal. The principal problem the team of researchers faced was the elimination of the self-destructive tendencies of this mutation, and absolute control of its rapid cell division.

Days of patient trial and error were needed before the team found itself on the edge of a breakthrough. Dr. Thornton refused to discuss those trials in detail when announcing his result: like the final equation that spelled out success in unmistakable terms, he felt they should remain the team's shared secret.

"The important fact is the equation itself," he said. "Plus the fact that its implementation is now both simple and practical. Batteries of solar convertors, set up in concentrated areas, can now be seeded in a few minutes' time. Once the process is standardized, harvests can be produced at a speed that will seem astounding to the layman. Using the method that proved its worth at Muong Toa, it will soon be possible to produce enough food to feed the whole world on less than a half-million acres. In sober fact, we are on the verge of a millennium when no man need go hungry again.

"In concrete terms," Dr. Thornton added, "the finished product need cost no more than a few cents a pound when raw waste is used as the principal fuel—which is the custom in the Orient. Even with other means of combustion, the cost would no more than double."

The journalist opened the notebook to a fresh page and took up his pencil. His voice was hoarse as he finished his recital. The glance that traveled from Chan to John and back again was almost avid.

"So much for the Muong Toa story, gentlemen," he said. "My dispatch still needs a news-peg for tomorrow. What's the next step?"

"Another test run, of course," said Chan. "A really large-scale run, using several convertors. I plan to stage it in Kunming."

During the reading, John had sat hunched above his notebook, verifying Chan's points as mechanically as a student at a graduate seminar. Throughout, he had continued to hope against hope that escape would somehow be possible—to insist, with what shaky logic he could muster, that Chan would keep his word. Now, with that illusion shattered, he was careful to hold his tongue. Chan's last remark had been addressed to Wilde direct. The pretense of an interview was still valid.

The journalist's pencil was racing to prison the final quote: John could see that even Lex was nonplused as he took down the words. It was Dud Porter's voice that cut the fog of silence.

"Did you say *Kunming?* In Yunnan Province?"

Chan turned to the technician with perfect courtesy.

"It's the nearest Chinese city with complete facilities. You'll find it suits our needs."

"What do you have in mind?"

"What I just told Mr. Wilde—the first massive production of algal powder by this method, and its first real testing, at all levels of the economy."

Dud moved a step forward, steadying himself with one hand on the table.

"This noon, when I showed you what John had done to the convertor, you promised us transport to Chiang Mai."

"That was before I contacted Dr. Yu on the shortwave." Chan faced John for the first time. "I *did* mean to keep our bargain. Unfortunately, Yu thinks we'll get optimum results in China."

Again, Dud Porter cut in swiftly. This time, the words were bellowed.

*"If you think we'll buy this sellout—!"*

"I don't like that last word, Doctor."

"What other should I use?"

"Surely there's nothing drastic in my proposal."

"You know we've no visas for Kunming."

"We've gone a bit beyond passport visas," said Chan. "Indra understands me perfectly. So, I'm sure, does John. Why can't you?"

John held up his hand to still the war of voices. "Let's have the whole plan, please."

174

The younger Thornton had been toying with a steel mallet as he continued to sit (with complete assurance) at the head of the worktable. Now, leaning forward, he struck a quick blow against a retort. The effect of the bell-like summons was startling. At first view the two figures bursting from the concealment of the mice-run seemed unreal as tattered mannequins. So did the automatic rifles they carried, the identical cold eyes beneath the comical hats they were wearing. Before they moved to cover the door, John recognized the two litter-bearers who had brought in the wounded Kha.

"Call them my couriers, if you like—or my bodyguards," said Chan. "You'll find them efficient on both counts."

John spoke quickly, above Dud's gasp of rage.

"Is this your notion of persuasion?"

"I think it's convincing," said Chan. "Don't you agree, Mr. Wilde?"

Lex had torn a dozen sheets from his notebook. Now, he thrust the untidy mass in his pocket and bounced to his feet. The heavy, bulldog figure had never seemed more tenacious, never more certain of its goal.

"Are you kidnapping *me* as well, Thornton?"

"Transport will arrive at any moment," said Chan. "I hope you'll join us willingly."

"After what you've just confessed?"

"You can round out your story in Kunming and file it from there. After it's been checked for accuracy, of course."

"I'm sending *this* dispatch from Thailand," said the journalist. "You aren't the first Commie roadblock I've broken."

"Don't test this one, Mr. Wilde. You'll regret it."

Lex charged toward the door, with the head-down momentum of a linebacker who has just intercepted a fumble. John held his breath as the two runty guards seemed on the point of yielding. Then, at Chan's soft-voiced command, a gun-butt rose and fell, dropping Wilde in his tracks.

In the silent room, the thud of steel on bone had a sickening finality. John dropped a hand to Dud Porter's shoulder before he could go to the journalist's aid.

"The message's registered, Chan," he said.

The younger Thornton had not stirred from the table.

Watching the guards drag Lex to the far wall and prop him there, he seemed unaware of John's words.

"That was a truly futile gesture," he said. "I thought our friend Wilde was a pragmatist. Apparently, he's a boy scout at heart."

"You could have killed him."

"My men are experts. He'll have a slight concussion, nothing more. When he's revived, he'll write what he's told to write."

"Do you think you can manage a free press so easily?"

"Your Mr. Wilde is no longer free, John. His by-line is still valuable. That's why he's flying back with us, in Dr. Yu's hospital plane."

"Are you really shifting your base—along with your loyalties?"

"Our move to Kunming is part of a larger pattern. One that's been planned for some time. At this point, I'm not permitted to tell you the details."

"You're giving Yu our equation to use as he sees fit?"

"That was my intention from the start."

"Won't you pinpoint our whereabouts—if you file a news story from Kunming, under Wilde's by-line?"

"The pinpointing is deliberate, John. In a few days, your Stateside friends will hear we've delivered what Dr. Porter calls the 'Food Bomb' to the People's Republic. Naturally those friends will suspect you were abducted. They'll sing another tune when we submit our first paper to the *International Journal of Microbiology*. It will tell just how we joined forces with Dr. T. K. Yu, to banish famine in China—"

"And you think I'll approve such procedure?"

"We'll sign that paper together—as co-workers. Like it or not, our names will go down in history as the greatest benefactors the yellow race has known."

"Will China share the discovery with others?"

"That's more than I can answer now. Dr. Yu plans to detonate the first food bomb in Yunnan. I won't pretend that two mere biologists like ourselves can control its explosions thereafter—" The younger Thornton held up his hand for silence. High above the roof, the throb of a jet plane's motors had just set the shutters trembling.

No one moved in the alcove while the plane circled the kampong, then came into the wind for its landing. Chan was the first to rise from the table. With a short warning to the guards, he moved to the west wall of the lab, to open the window nearest the airstrip.

The white-winged Chinese hospital plane had just eased to a stop on the tarmac, with its nose facing the hangar. While John watched, the door was opened and a file of uniformed guards poured out. There were ten in all. Each man carried an automatic rifle at port arms: like performers in some macabre ballet, they moved quickly to ring the ship with steel. Expecting Yu to end the procession, John felt his spirits sink as the maneuver ended. The fact that Chan had unmasked so insolently was numbing enough. Now it was evident the agronomist had trusted him to close his trap unaided.

Chan turned to face the group again. "I think that completes the pattern of my intentions," he said easily. "It's obvious I'm prepared to enforce them. Are there any questions?"

"Dud asked you to explain your sellout," John said. "I'm asking you again."

"There's been no sellout. Look back on events with an open mind. Haven't I been entirely honest—ever since you arrived here?"

"You lied about the road to the Gates."

"I told you the People's Republic was building there. Is it important if the construction was a road, or a power dam? Southeast Asia was marked as our province when the French left Indochina."

"Did you say *our*?" Indra asked.

"Do you blame me so much for moving with history?"

"History may write a different ending."

"Don't cloud your mind with sentiment, Indra. Most men are happiest when they take orders from a master. Why

177

should it matter if it's a benign ruler like my father—or a farseeing discipline that can *really* remake the world?"

"Is your faith that absolute?"

"In China's four-thousand-year misery, it's always been the story of ruler and slave—whether the ruler's the Great Khan, a feeble Manchu emperor, or a twentieth-century warlord. Today, at last, China's clay has been shaped by hands that know their job. I'm proud to join the molders."

"Suppose you find you're being molded too?" John asked.

"It's happened many times before."

"Not with friends like Dr. Yu to assure my advancement. And particularly not when I bring a perfect molding tool with me."

John cast a look into the deepening shadows of the lab. Dud Porter, a patient worker to the end, had moved to stoke the jet burner. The two guards had resumed their posts at the outer door, where Lex Wilde (slumped like a meal sack against the wall) showed no signs of reviving. The inventory was a mechanical one. Even now, he realized, he was still playing instinctively for time: he could hardly have explained why.

"Let's skip the dogma of your masters," he said. "Judging by what you've just told Indra, you've been one of them for some time."

"I joined the Party after Dr. Yu's first visit."

"Was your father aware of your choice?"

"My father was a misguided idealist. It seemed kinder to let him leave this world with his illusions."

"Whose idea was it, using his illness to bring me here?"

"Mine, John. I admitted as much, the day of your arrival." With his eyes on the airstrip, Chan moved to put a hand on John's shoulder, vetoed the impulse, and thrust both hands into the pockets of his lab coat. "You'd been here only a few hours when I told you—quite openly—that I accepted accident cases from across the border. Later, I described the visits of Dr. Yu in some detail—including the help he'd given with my lab supplies. I even confessed I'd share the equation with him, if your notions had been less adamant."

"You never confessed you were outright allies."

"You never asked me. Nor did I mention that a certain Dr. Sung, a Taiwan scientist whose real home was Shanghai, had lifted algal cultures from your San Francisco workroom." Chan glanced toward the convertor, and Dud's black-browed scowl. "As you see, each move of our gambit was thought out beforehand, with *almost* complete candor as the guiding principle. The trap was expertly baited, John. I must say you rose dutifully to the lure."

"I take it the bait was Yu's idea?"

Chan shook his head. "That was mine too. So was the timing. T. K. Yu is a patient man, but I can't say as much for his superiors. While our tests hung fire here, they asked that you be arrested at once. *I* held out for the brotherhood of science. Now my patience has paid off, to say nothing of my apparent frankness. *You* were deceived completely—after those first intelligent doubts. So was our hand-me-down Confucius Prince Ngo Singh. So was your chowderheaded journalist—"

"Are you sure you haven't underestimated some of us?"

"I think not. We go to Kunming as a team—and our goal is a virtual reality. Give me six months—and I'll prove how well we can serve the People's Republic—"

"Will you serve the rest of Asia?" Indra asked.

"Not until China has established her right to rule there. At this moment, my mutation belongs to my adopted country alone. With luck, the secret will remain in our hands for years. While that happy state endures, we'll use it as a club to bring countries like India in line. Even if the West resorts to nuclear war, we can lose five hundred million dead—and feed our survivors in the ashes."

"Now we've done our job," said John, "I suppose Dud and I will be early casualties."

"Not necessarily. If you'll see the light, you could be invaluable. Eventually, we might even return you to the States. That's a hope, not a promise."

"And Indra?"

The girl's head lifted. John could read the patient surrender in her eyes.

179

"I'm sure our captor's thoughts are explicit where I'm concerned," she murmured.

"You've stated the case admirably," Chan said. "At the start, you were an added attraction to bring John here. You continued to believe in me with a devotion I found touching. You persuaded John to stay on, as eloquently as Ngo Singh. For those reasons, I've decided to spare your life—"

"Does that mean I'll stay in Muong Toa?"

"I said I'd *spare* you, Indra. Not that I'd set you free. If you'd loved me, I'd have made you my wife long ago. Instead, you chose John. I must exact a penalty for that lapse of taste. Tonight, after we reach Kunming, I'm sending you to a coolies' brothel."

Indra seized John's arm before he could fling himself at Chan.

"We've had enough violence here," she said. "May I board the plane? I'm beginning to find this situation trying."

"As well you might," said Chan. He had ignored John's fury, with the same maddening calm. "You, at least, are a fatalist: John's amazement is a trifle overdue. Only a great fool, or a great idealist, could have failed to suspect my intentions. I'll grant him the second category in return for past favors."

"You've had your pound of flesh, Chan," said Indra. "Isn't it time to go?"

"I'm staying until this last test run ends. When we close up shop here, our reports must be complete." Chan's tone was almost apologetic, as his eyes roamed round the table. "Someone must remain with the convertor until its final yield is recorded. The rest may board the plane at once, if it will ease Indra's feelings."

No one spoke while the girl marched through the outer door with her head high. At Chan's order, the taller of the two coolies lifted the still-inert journalist to one shoulder, and followed her. The second guard fell into step behind.

"*One* of you may come aboard when he wishes," Chan said. "The other must stay until the run is ended. I won't mention the futility of escape, or other hostile acts. After all, I have hostages to insure your good behavior."

The door clanged shut on Chan's departure, granting the two remaining occupants of the lab a tenuous privacy. Dud left the jet burner promptly, and moved to the valves of the convertor.

"We can still outsmart him, Boss. Remember how things backfired, the first time you were alone here?"

"There'll be no repeat performance, Dud."

"I've set the stage. The methane intake to the furnace is shut off. Give this old girl her head, and she'll build up gas like a sick whale. A lighted match would do the trick."

"Chan wants one of us to stay. The other must board the plane. *You're* elected, my friend."

"You should go first, to be with Indra."

"Not when you have the death wish and an itching hand."

"Which would you rather be? A cinder today, or a zombie tomorrow?"

"Haul tail to that plane, Dud, and do it now. That's an order."

The iron in John's tone was enough to send Dud from the lab. Watching his slow departure, he did not go to the convertor to adjust the methane valve. Instead, he found himself moving (like a man in a waking dream) to light a Bunsen burner near the alcove door, to place a twisted newspaper beside it, to pull the doors half-shut, until the labored breathing of the *bat jhow yee* was muted.

Even now, he realized he was obeying a need that transcended logic. When one of the two armed coolies strode into the lab and took a rack of mutation culture from the incubator, he found he could return to his notebooks as coolly as though years of patient research lay ahead.

For the next quarter-hour, a procession of guards marched through each room, stripping the worktables of their equipment with a skill that suggested rehearsal. Forcing himself to ignore the intruders, John found it easy to feign a concentration on his note-taking, now that his mind had settled on a course of action. Twice in that quarter-hour, he returned to the alcove to siphon excess methane from the tubes, lest the the event he planned occur ahead of schedule. The moves were made automatically; Chan, he felt sure, would trust him

181

to tabulate the last Chlorella harvest in Muong Toa. What happened thereafter would depend on luck—and his own courage.

He was still correcting his notes when the outer door swung open again. Long before he heard the click of the closing padlock, he knew it was Chan. Turning to face his enemy, John was startled to find that a heavy rain was falling in the compound.

The younger Thornton, a mackintosh tossed over his shoulders, strode to the incubator to lift out another case of culture tubes. "We'll take an extra rack of the mutation," he said. "It'll mean a head start in Kunming tomorrow."

"Is it time to take off?"

"I think so. With the weather breaking, there's no point in continuing the run."

John kept both hands on the master-notebook. He was still bemused by his freedom from tension—now he could measure his life (and Chan Thornton's) in minutes.

"Not that it concerns me," he said, "but how will the compound function when you abandon it?"

"Vong will take charge, I suppose."

"Wouldn't it be simpler to cut him down?"

"I discussed that with Dr. Yu. We decided it was too soon for bloodshed in the Valley."

"I suppose this way is neater, now you mention it."

"Neater—and much simpler. You've played for time long enough, John. Hand over that notebook, please."

"You'll have to come and get it."

Chan circled the table slowly, a move which John paralleled. When they stood face-to-face down its length, John saw that an automatic pistol was nested in his enemy's palm.

"As you see," said Chan, "I've anticipated this defiance. I also have a fair idea of your activities this last quarter-hour. First, you'd shut the methane valve—so those tubes would be filled to bursting when I returned. *Then*, of course you planned a well-staged explosion that would destroy us both—"

"Such was my hope," John said. He let his hands slide downward with the words, until both were anchored at the table's rim.

Chan glanced toward the half-open alcove. "A lighted Bunsen burner," he said softly. "A paper torch beside it. You planned well, John. Unfortunately, I've decided to end things my own way. Just one death is in prospect this afternoon—your own."

Holding his enemy's eyes, John forced out the final irony. "Aren't we partners any more?"

"You aren't the type for brainwashing. Once you've surrendered that notebook, I can dispense with your services."

"Methane's already begun to seep into the room. If I were you, I'd turn off the burner."

Chan swung toward the flame. Before he could turn back, John had upended the table pinning him to the laboratory wall. Using the table as an impromptu shield, he raced for the shelter of the next aisle. In the same move, he let his hand brush the wall, snapping the light switch and filling the room with shadows, now that the downpour outside had shut off the sun.

The zinc-plated boards of the worktable deflected Chan's first hasty shot. Before he could fire again, John had reached the haven of the mice-run. From that plywood maze, it was only a dozen strides to the room's west wall. The window Chan had opened was fitted with a wire grille, and the fugitive saw he could not dislodge it. The open steel shutters made a fair hiding place. Not daring to face toward the airstrip, he stood with his back to the screen, ready to dodge if his enemy discovered his whereabouts.

The Bunsen burner had been forgotten in Chan's compulsive need to hunt him down. For a moment more, he continued to charge from aisle to aisle, in a furious effort to seek out his quarry. When a fusillade of rifle fire swept the kampong, it seemed to explode inside John's head.

The volley had been short and vicious: still without turning, he sensed that it had come from the airstrip. At first he was positive his companions had been shot down on order; the ensuing silence, and Chan's gasp of surprise, told a different story. Somehow, he knew, the guards had been ambushed and cut down. There could be no other meaning to

183

Chan's rush for the outer door, his frantic fumble for the key that would turn the padlock.

The respite gave John a belated chance to face the airstrip. Prepared, in a sense, for what had occurred there, he still hardly dared to believe what he saw.

When he had first peered through this screen, the plane had been ringed by quilted uniforms. Now, the ten guards were tumbled on the earth like sawdust dolls. Chan's two coolie commandos lay dead beside them. A group of Meo tribesmen, armed with antique machine guns, had just burst from the hangar, ready for a needless *coup de grâce*. While John continued his staring, a second wave of the same lethal ambush, led by the tall figure of Fa Ngoum, ran from the hospital wing to mass at the plane door.

There was no further sound as the two pilots emerged rashly, ran for their lives, and fell in a welter of flashing knife blades.

Chan, still fumbling for his key, gave a strangled cry when the door was kicked open from the outside. Prince Ngo Singh stood on the threshold, his cassock tucked into a pair of GI trousers, an M-1 rifle at the ready.

"The invasion was a failure, Chan," he said calmly. "It's time you surrendered."

*"No, damn you!"*

The words had burst from Chan's throat in a scream; he fired as he whirled toward the alcove—and the open court beyond. Again he had had no time to aim carefully: the bullet buried itself in the doorframe, above the Prince's head. Ngo Singh's answering shot struck Chan in the right shoulder, staggering him—and forcing him to drop the automatic from a suddenly nerveless hand. John saw that his eyes had swept the room wildly, in search of an exit. A second later, he had seized the twist of paper beside the Bunsen burner and ignited it in the flame.

"Don't shoot again," he warned the Prince—and his voice was steady with purpose now. "We'll die together, if I touch those solar tubes."

As he spoke, Chan backed toward the alcove. He could not see what was apparent to John. One of the tentacles of the

184

*bat jhow yee,* distended to the bursting point by its load of methane, was now slowly deflating. The reason was obvious. The bullet that had torn the muscles of Chan's shoulder had winged on to puncture the tubing, pouring a stream of gas into the alcove. In a matter of seconds its concentration in that narrow space would reach the detonation point.

"Don't try to get away, Chan—!"

John's shouted warning came too late. With the paper torch held high, Chan had already backed into the alcove, using his uninjured shoulder to shut the sliding doors behind him.

The explosion came just as John launched himself at the Prince, in a flying tackle that sent them both sprawling in a nest of worktables. Because Chan was already closing the doors from the inside, the force of the blast slammed them shut, sealing the main laboratory from much of the detonation. It was still violent enough to burst the south wall of the building, to send the convertor skyward in a geyser of flame and splintered glass.

Chan Thornton had simply vanished in that spout of red. Only a gaping crater remained to mark the spot where the food bomb had been born.

"I'd have warned you sooner, if I could," said the Prince. "My beginning of wisdom, I fear, came just in time."

"Let's thank your son for that, Sir—and the force he trained in the caves."

"It shames me to say it now, Doctor, but only yesterday we quarreled over that training. I feared it would provoke our enemies."

John and Ngo Singh were seated in the cabin of the captured hospital plane. Indra, at the controls, had just finished revving the engines. On the tarmac, the farewell gestures of Dr. Vong were backed by the cheers of a half-hundred Meo tribesmen, led by Prince Fa Ngoum. It made a garish coda to their deliverance: John accepted it dazedly.

"Surely there'll be some reprisal, Your Highness."

"Perhaps not. What have they given up, besides this plane?"

"We're leaving twelve dead commandos on the airstrip. To say nothing of two pilots."

"Life is cheap in the People's Republic," said Ngo Singh. "Let's call those fourteen victims pawns in a never ending game."

"And Chan?"

"A knight born under an evil star."

"Does it seem strange to be an active player again?"

"Strange—and oddly refreshing," said the Prince. "I have watched from the sidelines too long. Now, it seems, I must organize a government the world can respect. My materials are waiting in exile."

"What of your son?"

"He will be needed—to represent me in the Valley. To organize a guerilla army, if we are attacked. As you saw today, he has some small aptitude for the task."

The plane had lifted from the tarmac while they talked. Both of them stared down at the Enchanted Valley—beginning to glow in fresh greens, now the rainsquall had lifted. Already, the kampong and its village were a blur below the wings. Only a smoke plume marked the gutted walls of Chan Thornton's lab.

"You're sure we can fly to Thailand?" John asked.

"My son arranged everything, Doctor. On the shortwave."

John's glance moved to the plane's cabin. It was crowded with stacks of equipment from the lab, a brace of Meo gunners seated at the cargo ports, and the shakedown bed for Lex Wilde, who had just sat up groggily, to fumble for his typewriter as a drunkard might reach for his bottle. Dud Porter, who had been making an inventory of their precious freight, came forward with the list.

"How's it feel to breathe again, Boss?"

"It's coming hard, but I'll manage."

The assistant lifted a familiar notebook from his pocket and opened it to a set of figures the microbiologist knew by heart.

"What shall we do with this?"

John took the dog-eared record from Dud's hand. It was their completed equation, the harnessing factors that would put the mutation of *Chlorella Thorntoni* in bondage for all time. The food bomb, he reflected, far from saving lives on

186

a less than perfect planet, had already been responsible for fifteen deaths. Yielding to impulse, he ripped the equation from the book, touched a match to its corner and watched it burn to ash.

"Wouldn't you call this our safest course, Your Highness?"

"I would, Doctor," said Ngo Singh. "At least, until we reach the protection of a friendly government. You have cultures of the mutation, of course?"

"They were the first item the Chinese brought aboard."

"Can you and Dr. Porter rewrite the equation from memory?"

"In our sleep, Sir," said Dud.

"We'll do the writing in Washington," John added.

"In the office of your President?"

"Have we another choice?"

"Why not the Secretariat of the United Nations?" the Prince asked. "Or the World Health Organization?"

"Sorry—no more gambles." John looked down at the crumbling ash. "If you hadn't saved us when you did, this could have been a devil's harvest."

"A *devil's* harvest, Dr. Merchant?"

"Yes—in the wrong hands. China has sown its dragon's teeth before—if you'd prefer another metaphor. This time, if Chan had had his way, the dragon might have torn the earth apart."

The copilot's seat beside Indra was empty. When John settled there, she gave him a faint smile of welcome.

"Why are we still circling the Valley?" he asked.

"The Prince asked me to set that course. Does your watch match mine?"

"It's almost five."

"This is our last turn. Keep your eyes on the Gates of Hell. They're about to justify their name."

John leaned closer to the copilot's window. The plane had banked above Butterfly Mountain, to complete a long turn to the northeast. Eight thousand feet below, the lichened walls of the monastary had just come into view. Beyond, the twin ramparts of the Gates lifted starkly from their jungle base.

John saw that Indra had drawn his attention to those ramparts none too soon. On the stroke of five, as precisely as though a magician had touched them with his wand, the two monoliths seemed to dissolve. In a space of seconds, they had crumbled into rubble above the narrow defile that formed the only entrance to the Valley.

"Chan didn't have a monopoly on destruction," the girl said calmly.

The completed circle had carried them well above the explosion. Even so, there was a faint shiver in the fuselage as the concussion's wave reached them. Far below, the teak forest had begun to burn brightly. Now that the dust cloud was thinning, John saw that massive rockslides had wiped the defile from view, creating a rampart no bulldozer could breach.

"Fa Ngoum insisted you see it," said Indra. "He's proud of his record as a demolition expert."

"No wonder the caves were guarded."

"He's been storing explosives there for months." Indra set the plane's course due south, then surrendered control to the automatic pilot. Her hand already closed on John's as the jet settled on its course to Chiang Mai. "Mr. Wilde once said it was ironic that the Gates of Hell should guard the Enchanted Valley. He was a better prophet than he knew. Now they've been destroyed, they'll *really* guard it—forever."